Goodbye Georgia

By

Jana Godshall

ISBN 1-4033-3621-0 (e-book)
ISBN: 1-4033-3622-9 (Paperback)
ISBN: 1-4033-3623-7 (Dustjacket)

This book is printed on acid free paper.

1stBooks - rev. 10/25/02

ACKNOWLEDGEMENTS

I would like to thank God for giving me strength.

Thanks to mom and dad for supporting me in everything I do, and for always being right by my side.

There is no way I could have ever completed this novel if it had not been for Ernest Gaines. Not only was it his inspiration, but it was also is encouraging and profound words.

I would also like to thank Ray Powers for his unbelievable faith and support in me for if it were not for his devout confidence in me I may have given up on hope.

And lastly, but certainly not least, to my friends for always being able to inspire me.

Table of Contents

About the Book

Writing. . .when in my life did I think I would like writing? Actually, I have no idea. I was fifteen when I finished <u>Goodbye Georgia</u>, and how it all started…well, it is even a bit of a mystery to me. What started off as a journal entry soon developed into a book. Thoughts and ideas, confusion and frustration all led me to complete my first novel.

I was first introduced to slavery as a little girl. As I recall, it was somewhat of a family event; we gathered around the television every night to watch the mini-series, "Roots." The characters somehow never left my heart as I was growing up, and I guess it somehow helped to inspire me. I remember my freshman year in high school I started writing about a character Isabel and her companion, Jones. Soon it became a story, a story that I never was able to live except in my heart. The relationships within this book are rare, so rare that most people will live their entire lives and never find a true soul mate. One thing that always bothered me was what people search for, but who am I to look down upon what other people search for in their lives. I think what I was realizing was maybe that I, too, was searching for the wrong things. People spend lifetimes in search for the wrong things. People search for love, and not that that is the wrong thing to search for because it isn't. Love needs to surround us, but people seem to only search for love with a person they can be physically involved with. Maybe, this is the cause of why so many people feel incomplete. Soon they'll settle for the next best because they've lost hope, and they no longer have the strength to search. I believe in the search, but not necessarily the same one. The character Isabel has searched and come across a soul mate, but not a physical lover, a true soul mate. Her soul mate is an elderly man, and they connect on levels lovers never could and that is what completes them…and maybe that is what completes all of us. We just forget what to search for. <u>Goodbye Georgia</u> is a story about love, about relationships, about freedom, and hope. If I had half the strength, moderation, and faith as Isabel, Jones, or Emma, another companion, then I would not be in battle with myself or with my own emotions.

This novel was written four years ago, and as I reread the words off the pages, I since a younger voice. A younger voice, that has much passion, and although the voice is younger, I would not describe it as naïve. I would describe it as youthful and hopeful, so hopeful that after four years I'm a little scared that I have lost some of that hope with my age. I fear sometimes that I will forget what is like to be young and free. Although I am quite a bit older than the character of Isabel, she is still a role model to me. She is someone I admire. I long for her youth; I long for her fearless strength; I long to find her companions.

I hope that in this novel you will capture what it is that I received and carry it with you for as long as you live. I don't like to give advice, and maybe you may be a little spectacle to receive advice from a girl of my age, but I will just say this one thing—never judge a person by their gender, age, or race but what it is that lies within their soul and just importantly be young forever…don't grow too old to fly.

Chapter 1

I suddenly awoke with a rush of energy. It felt as if I had been asleep for days. The mysterious place that I awoke had the sweet smell of wild strawberries. I didn't exactly know where I was, but I had some sort of an idea. Although, I didn't have a clue how I got there. The place was beautiful with every single color you could imagine in the color's perfect tint. I felt like I was living in a picture, an ideal place that never stopped glowing. Gold covered the ground I walked upon. The sky was dome of diamonds, and the walls were pictures of men and women with their name listed below, names of heroic and saintly people. My breath was taken away by all the beauty. Peace covered the land. The animals were calm and carefree. A lion was bathing a gazelle. I was barefoot, and as I walked forward, the gold soothed my feet. If I listened hard enough, I could hear a faint melody. The song was very familiar. I kept walking until I came upon a very large golden gate which was elegantly crafted. On the side of the gate, there stood before me a strong and fierce man. Although he was definitely elderly in the face, he shined like a young boy. He stared at me for a moment or two. I thought that I saw a grin, but it was immediately erased with a shake of his head.

"Name," The man said in a soothing voice.

"Excuse me, where am I exactly. I mean is this…" I was somewhat confused.

Cutting me off he said in the same soothing voice, "Your name please."

I nodded, "Isabel Climmings. Sir, could you kindly tell me… is this, wull is what I think it is?"

The man stared at me again for a good while and then looked down at the scroll he was holding in his hand. He then spoke, "Tell me your story." He could tell by the expression in my eyes that I needed him to elaborate. So he added, "Tell me the story of your life. Share your memories with me, Isabel." His words were so warm that you just wanted to lie down next to a fire.

I nodded once again. "Ok, my life story. Golly, let's see, where to begin... Wull, when I began to understand life and the people in my life, the meaning of words and the meaning of life, and started to realize why certain things happened, I was a young lady. Umm, I lived in Georgia on the most gorgeous plantation in those parts; it was the biggest, too. Oh, it was so beautiful." I closed my eyes remembering back...

I remember like it was yesterday — how the long grass would sway in the wind, the air always smelling of fresh lilies— I guess you could say it was somewhat magical. In the autumn, we would have the prettiest colored leaves you ever did see. There were yellows, reds, oranges, and even toasted golden browns. Even though some of my memories of the plantation were heartbreaking, the beauty surrounding my childhood home echoes in my soul even now.

My Paps was a man of no self respect. What I mean is he had to follow others. He didn't know how to be himself. Throughout my life, there was always someone like my Paps. Somebody who had to follow the crowd or somebody who had to be the richest and the best, even if deep down inside they weren't like that. I remember looking deep into my Paps eyes and sometimes I would think I saw some sort of light, some sort of hope. I don't recall if there was really any light, or if it was just a dream I wished upon. I do remember how he would always do something just awful to destroy that light that he might of had. Now for my Mama, wull, she was a woman who thought very highly of herself. She thought that money and power were the only way to happiness, as quite a few people do. She thought just because she was Daniel Wadsworth's wife that she could do anything she wanted. My Mama's mother lived with us, too, and I tried to get as little time as possible talking with her because speaking with that woman was as good as shooting a bullet through your head. And trust me, that's no side humor there; it's the darn near truth. For one thing my grandmother was a fake and phony in front of the other wealthy people. Here is an example of her perfect southern manners: "Oh darling, do take a seat. Isabel, honey, meet the lovely guests." And when the company finally left, it was like, "Isabel do this and that, and weren't those trashy good for nothing people just awful!" Because you see, no one- and I mean no one- was as good as my Grandma. My Grandma told me straight to my face that I was her least favorite person except for those niggers -sorry, pardon my language.

My Paps always wanted a boy and got one after my sister Sarah and I came along. Sarah was twenty around this time, and she had just gotten married to Charles O'Hara. They were going to build a little house in the back of the plantation, just so that they could get some peace and quiet away from everyone else. Paps said he was going to let Charles be part-owner in the plantation someday so there was really no use buying a place of their own since their future was with Wadsworth Estates. Sarah and Charles didn't know each other too well before they got married. And boy, they didn't have that much in common either. She had a hot temper and if you weren't aware of that it would knock you senseless.

My Paps got his wish ten years after me. It took awhile for my Mama to have another child because I was supposedly a lot to deal with and a long time to recover from. My Mama never let me forget that either. The little angel was named Joseph. He was spoiled rotten and no one seemed to mind but me. He thought that he could run crazy and say whatever he wanted. No one ever really taught him any better so I guess I can't put all the blame on him. It sometimes seemed like everyone was blind and deaf, and I was waving my arms and screaming on the top of my lungs for help and guidance or maybe even love but know one knew it.

Chapter 2

It was Monday, the nineteenth of May. On Mondays, Miss Laura came to teach me reading, writing, arithmetic, and all about the Bible. The reason Miss Laura came to our house was because the nearest school was a good hour by buggy and Paps didn't have the time to help get me there. And besides Mama said it was better this way. Miss Laura came to me on Mondays, Wednesdays, and Saturdays. She was one of the sweetest and most dearest people I knew. She was in some ways like another sister to me. I was very fortunate to have met her. The lessons she taught me, I have used the lessons she taught me all throughout my life-such as what to say in certain situations, what to expect from people, and even more importantly how to live each minute worthwhile. She taught me some of the most valuable lessons people only dream of getting taught.

It was eight o'clock, and Miss Laura would be at the house in a half hour. I always enjoyed the times she came. It was always something to look forward to. I didn't see her coming as just a time to learn, to me it was a time of adventure.

"Hello Mrs. Wadsworth, how's your morning so far?" Miss Laura said in a polite dainty voice.

"She's in the library," my Mama said in a rude and discomforting manner-no surprise to me. Miss Laura then gave my Mama a look of pity which wasn't the smartest thing to do. "Laura, we pay you to teach Isabel. So would you like to do that? Would you? Then go to the library!" Mama said. She wasn't exactly the best morning-person.

"Good day Mrs. Wadsworth," Miss Laura said in flustered voice. I suppose she was hoping she wouldn't see Mama on the way out.

Miss Laura came into the library a little blushed. I smiled at her, and she gave me one right back. She was a tall, thin, real purtty lady. That was one reason Mama felt awkward around her. Mama always had to be the most beautiful lady around. You could tell that she felt this way when you saw the people that she had over for tea. Mama was always jealous of someone. You see, Miss Laura really didn't look like most southern ladies. I guess different is always beautiful too, don't you think? I mean, when you keep looking at the same thing everywhere you go, it can get a little old and even boring. I guess that is why some people go on the outskirts just to be different.

"Isabel, Isabel, ISABEL!!!!" Miss Laura said frustratingly.

"Yes, sorry," I murmured.

"Honey, you are always daydreaming. Anything you want to tell me." I shrugged my shoulders. I really didn't know what I always seemed to dream too big — to unrealistically; things I dreamt about sometimes just seemed to silly to say aloud. Letting your mind wonder, go into space was something I always did. Usually the stuff I would dream about were always things just too unrealistic. Just too silly to say out loud.

Miss Laura shook her head and started laughing. "First things first, we need to work on your grammar. Isabel, it isn't used to your best ability. I know for a fact you can do better." One thing that I loved about Miss Laura was her way of critiquing because for one thing she put it in way which it wasn't a put-down. Also, she made you feel like you really could do much better.

"Now, let's get started." I tried to act like I was all into it to make her feel better.

"Alright, it is proper for a young lady like yourself to speak in a proper manner. Say *cannot, will not*, and *do not* to begin with. I said those words as enthusiastically as I could to make Miss Laura happy because she would think that I really liked this sort of stuff because I liked her. You know when you like or love someone you tend to do things the way that they like it. It may take a while for the person to notice, but if you keep pushing they'll soon learn that you love them.

After grammar came arithmetic and writing, then Bible studies. When Miss Laura was teaching me about the Bible and all the stories, she kept repeating how God loves each and every one of us so much. She also said if we make a mistake and sin that God would forgive us with no hard feelings. But when she said that he loved us all equally, it made me realize that God loved me the same as Mama, Paps, and that would mean Jones and Emma too. Jones and Emma were slaves on our plantation. If God loved them the same as Mama and Paps then what made my Mama and Paps any better? Nothing, nothing at all.

"Honey, it's twelve thirty; I'll be on my way. Now, for Wednesday I want you to write a paper about any Bible verse in the Old Testament, and also an essay on George Washington whom we talked about last week. Do you understand?" Miss Laura sounded pretty serious.

"Oh, yes ma'am. I'll have it done."

"Bye my sweet. I'll look forward to seeing you Wednesday," she said back in her normal sweet voice.

"Bye Miss Laura!" I shouted on her way out. She waved her hand as she floated away.

Chapter 3

I don't think I've told you already, but my absolute favorite parts of the plantation were the cornfields. They were beautiful and safe. While I was in the cornfields, no one could harm me. The stalks were our shields to protect us. I really don't know how else to explain it to you except that it was the closest thing to perfect at that time. I spent basically about all my time outside and half the time that I was outside I spent in the cornfields. It was like I could go free in there. I mean I could just let go. I would spread my arms as far as I could and just run free. People don't like to admit it, but we all let go and run free. Not everyone runs in the physical sense, but whether we run in our minds or physically we let everything go. We all forget about the worries even if it's just for a minute. Everyone has to tend to the hurt inside.

Since I lived on a plantation and my Paps owned it, you probably figured out that he was a planter. The richest one in the county too. And if you didn't know already, which you probably did, we had slaves and a lot for that matter. I tell you one thing, I'm not proud of that at all. I hate the fact that we were being cruel to others. When Paps or one of his hands would whip a slave, I wanted to ask them how they could do that to a human being. If you never saw it with your own eyes, you will never know the pain it caused. People need to see not with their minds but with their hearts. I would always tell myself that people were blind in a matter of speaking.

My family couldn't see past the color of someone's skin, but for some reason I could, or I just didn't care. When I first became friends with some of the slaves, I think I did it because I wasn't getting the attention I needed from my family. I needed someone I could really count everyday, someone I could open up to. There was always Miss Laura, but I only saw her a couple of hours three days a week. I needed more than that, and I didn't see the color. The closest friend of mine was an elderly black man, named Jones. Jones was tall, strong, and the gentlest man I ever met. He wouldn't hurt a fly. Some people would be a little frightened when they first saw Jones because he was fierce and his eyes were of daggers, but if you were lucky enough to speak with him, you would learn that he was as kind as they come. He was a very caring and compassionate man. I grasped every word he ever spoke because his words were so thought out and important. His words changed my life. I could share anything with him. I found it was very important to have that, someone that you could tell anything too. Jones and I had a lot in common; for one thing we felt the same way about the cornfields. Jones usually worked there in the cornfields, and we would always go to the cornfields together, just to be free. We taught each other so much about life and how everything works. Shoot, we did just everything together. One time Emma, another slave, said that we were like two peas in a pod. Emma taught me a lot of stuff to—like when something goes wrong not to sulk, and when I would fail at something keep my head high. She would say that I had to get up and not to let it happen again. She was a tough woman, but she had to be to survive. She had six children, and she didn't see one of them turn five. They were all sold before that. She had to learn not to get too attached to something because when you love something so much it's hell to watch it leave you. She told me to take nothing for granted. If it looks too good to be true she said that it probably was.

There were a lot of others at the plantation, but I wasn't as close to them as I was with Jones and Emma. There was Ole John, but everyone called him Ole Uncle. I never knew why we called him that, but someone started it and it just stuck. He was a heck of a nice man, strong as a bull too. Umm, there was Ticey and Cranby. They were married, but no one was really supposed to know because my Paps didn't allow marriage among the slaves. They had a little boy named Junior who must of been four or five by then. He was as cute as a button. Pete dealt with the buggies. I got to know him really well when he had to take me to town one day to get some linen for my Grandma. Charles was suppose to go with us, but he told me he had to have an important meeting with Sarah. He made me promise not to tell anyone that he snuck off. So it was just me and Pete, and we didn't stop talking the entire time there and back. He was such a funny man. He looked at everything bad and tried to put laughter into it. I never saw him without a smile. Oh and of course, there was Lily and Ann who worked inside. They would cook our meals, wash the clothes, and make sure everything was spick-and-span inside. Lily always made sure I was clean and on time for the meals. She always watched out for me like that. She was the one who tucked me into bed the way I liked it. Lily could of been anywhere from late thirties to her early forties. She was short and chubby—the opposite of Ann who was tall and bony. Ann was younger than Lily, but I didn't recall her age. In fact, hardly any of the slaves knew their exact age because they either didn't know how to count or they lost count as the years went by. There were tons more slaves, but I wasn't close to all of them as I was—no still am—with the ones I told you about. The ones that I mentioned are the ones who were special to me, who taught me something helpful in my journey of life.

Now, I don't want you getting the idea in your head that I hate my Mama. True, we're different and don't get along all the time but there was never hate. I know that my Mama had to of tried and that is why I love her. I know she never really spent a nickel of her money on me, but money is not the way to happiness. You just have to look at the real meaning of life. When I grew older, I always looked back and wished that I had had a better relationship with my Mama. I would always envy Sarah because she could talk with Mama the way I could only dream of. They would sit and talk for hours the way a mother and daughter should. I knew jealousy was wrong, but it was only natural for a girl to be upset. It was so hard to be nice to Sarah after her and Mama just spent the whole afternoon talking to one another because I was probably jealous. I supposed Mama didn't have much in common with me. Heck, to be honest I could say we were total opposites. I loved the outdoors while she preferred having tea on white doilies in the pallor. She told me none too few times that I was a contrarian.

I would always just close my eyes and just dream. I often dreamt about living in a different world where there would be no favoritism or hatred. I would wonder what the future would be like and if it would still have the hatred. The answer is sadly yes. That a world without hate is… wull it's only heaven.

Chapter 4

It was a beautiful Wednesday morning; you couldn't imagine such a sweet day. I had just finished my breakfast in the dinning room when I heard Miss Laura knock on the door.

Charles answered the door, "You look as lovely as usual Laura. How have you been these past few days? Good, I hope." Charles spoke in such a attractive voice like he was trying to impress Miss Laura because even Sarah noticed something strange about the voice he was using. Wull, the fact that he answered the door was strange. He never answered the door; it was supposedly the slaves' job to do that.

"Fine, thank you. I hope that you are doing just as well. Charles I figured you would be in the fields by now. Are you feeling well?"

"Fine, fine just running a little late. Good seeing you Laura."

"Oh, I guess I'll see you later." Miss Laura said totally charmed walking towards the library with Charles's eyes following her.

Sarah was listening to the entire conversation very intensely. I could picture the jealousy in Sarah's eyes, the fire burning. You know, it wasn't even that big of a deal, but Sarah took everything to the third degree.

"Charlie!" Sarah said in an angered loud voice.

"What, darling? What's wrong?" Charles said in an innocent way.

"Don't give me that, *what's wrong*! You know exactly what's wrong. You and that Laura are what's wrong!!!"

"Honey, I was just being polite to the lady. You know that you are the only girl for me," Charles said trying to smooth things over.

"Charlie," Sarah said still being firm.

"Look angel, I love you and you are the only one I will ever love." Charles's voice could win the heart of any girl.

"Wull, good." Sarah said almost in tears. Don't ask why. She would probably cry if it rained. She was always crying it seemed like. And over the silliest things, nothing of real importance. That was the total opposite of me. I never cried.

"Is that all, darling?" Charles said rubbing her shoulders.

With a sigh she replied, "I love you too."

As she was walking away, he grabbed her arm and turned her around and kissed her. Then I knew that Sarah forgot the whole thing about Miss Laura. I would sometimes wonder if Charles meant anything he said because he could sure talk his way out of everything.

Miss Laura walked in the door with a friendly greeting, "Hello, Isabel hon."

"Wull, hello Miss Laura. How ya' be?" Miss Laura quickly erased her grin with a frown and said in a firm manner, "Isabel, it is said properly—*Good morning Miss Laura. How are you doing?*"

"Yes'm." I repeated twice with no reason.

"Your mama will not be happy with me if you keep repeatedly talking this way. In fact, hon, she would ask me to stop coming."

"Of course she wouldn't do that Miss Laura. You're talking nonsense." I tried saying in the most assuring voice that I could but it's true you never knew with Mama.

Changing the subject she said, "Well the papers better be just about perfect, Izzy."

"Oh, Miss Laura, you will be so pleased with all of my work." I tried to put my words together as proper and ladylike as I could. And I thought that I was getting better at talking properly. She didn't say anything afterwards so I didn't know if I was really improving. Don't you just hate that, when you try your hardest and no one notices. Wull, it might seem like that sometimes, but trust me someone does notice you. They might not tell you, but they notice. When you feel that you have done something good and nobody seems to notice, I have learned that you have to have confidence in yourself. I had to teach this lesson to myself, living the kind of life I lived... Listen, people aren't always going to be there for you, telling you to keep trying or to push harder. You have to do that much on your own.

"Isabel, Isabel, listen up, "Miss Laura had been fixing all the mistakes in my papers. I guess that there was a lot cause she didn't look too impressed with my writings. I mean does it really matter how many mistakes there are if the words you put down were from the heart and really and truly meant something.

"Yeah, I mean, yes, Miss Laura," I said very awkwardly.

"Honey, you can't start sentences with words like, "cause" or "ain't" or "and" or even "gonna." You have to have specific subjects to start off with. You can't put sentences together. You have to use periods, semicolons, or conjunctions."

Miss Laura lectured me the rest of the time. I think from now on I'll try my hardest. to talk and write properly. She gave me about ten assignments on writing. 'Bout three in religion, two in arithmetic, and one book to read. The book had a strange title. It was called the <u>Odyssey</u>, which meant a long journey.

"I'm off," Miss Laura said. Her voice was back to its normal self again.

"Bye, Miss Laura."

"Izzy, please don't look at me like that. Listen, honey, I'm sorry; I'm just not in the best of moods today, you understand?" Miss Laura's voice was sweet yet sorrowful which made me feel bad, and made me think- was I giving her a funny look?

"I want you to finish this work by Saturday. Oh and Isabel, I'll have to come a half hour early on Saturday because I have to leave a half hour early. I have a big family dinner at 12:30 on Saturday. I'll have just enough time to get there if I leave thirty minutes early."

"Yes'm, I'll see you on Saturday at eight," I said it very slowly so I spoke in a perfect southern way.

"Bye, my sweet."

"Bye," I said relieved that she left in a good mood. I hate it when you leave and someone is mad or something ain't right because then you'll have this guilt just hanging on you. Guilt is not something you just want to hand out to others. It just makes me sick.

Miss Laura told me once to make others feel guilty is the devil talking. Miss Laura left with Sarah right by the door so this time Sarah could make sure nothing happened even though by this time, Charles was outside.

"Good day, Sarah." Miss Laura said trying to push over the idea that she was sorry for having upset her.

I think that Sarah got the idea so she said, "And to you Miss Laura." She said it like she wasn't even upset to begin with. But Sarah is a good tricker. Wull, I mean she can act like she is not bothered by something when she really is. I was never really able to that. Sarah told me being difficult to understand is all a part of being a lady. I never understood it. I smiled when I was happy, frowned when I was sad, and said yes when I wanted something and no when I didn't. I wasn't about to change any of that just because it came along with being a female.

Chapter 5

"Izzy, Izzy, where you be Izzy? I could faintly hear the sound of dear Lily's voice. She is one of the slaves that I mentioned earlier.

"Lily, I'm in here." Lily always made me smile. I mean she was so full of energy, and she was so sweet. She was more tender than a peach and softer than a swab of cotton.

"Oh, there you is. There you is. Izzy, I beens lookin' fer ya'. Yer Ma and Pa wants ya' in da dining room fa dinner. Yer Ma ain't in a good moods so ya' best go right now guh," she said curling her lip and pointing her finger at me. I stood up to go and Lily said, "Whatcha wearing guh? Why in da heavens did ya' change afta breakfast? Ya' was wearin' a pretty dress, now you wearing a torn ole thing. Ya' gottas go change, cause if yer Ma saw ya' wearing dose clothes she darn have a fit. Goes put on da dress dat ya' was wearin' dis mornin'. Go on upstairs, I'm right behind ya'.

"Yes Lily," I responded.

I was wearing a very old dress with the seam undone and the lace falling off. I do suppose it was inappropriate. The reason I changed into a different dress after breakfast was because that one was much more comfortable. It seems like I've always had that dress. It was kinda like that old teddy bear you have, you can't get rid of because it has too much sentimental meaning behind it. It brings back way too many memories to just throw away.

When I walked into my room, the sun was peeking in from the square window in the left corner. Against my window, I had my bed with my white quilt rested on top which was made by my great-grandmother. Over in the right corner of my room, I had my dressers and mirror. The two dressers were made from the finest woods. The shorter of two had a mirror at the top and a stool below where I could sit and brush my hair while staring into the mirror. Back then my hair touched my back and it was the brightest and shiniest auburn hair you ever did see. It was my favorite part of me, in the physical sense. I would never dream of cutting it. Lily was grabbing the dress that I had on earlier out of the closet.

"Here ya' go Izzy," Lily said in her high little voice.

"Thanks, Lily." I said as I reached for the dress out of her arms. It was a pretty dress; it was a long baby blue dress with white trim. It was short sleeve and very plain, but most of dresses were plain because my Mama never really cared if my dresses were fancy or not. It never bothered me any. I was fine with whatever.

"Hurry! Izzy ya gots'ta hurry! Dinners ready and ya Ma ain't happy." Lily spoke so fast I could barely make out what she was saying.

"I'm hurrying. I'm hurrying," I said.

As she ran down the stairs to the dining room, I hurried and put on my dress forgetting my shoes. I ran down the wooden stairs into the dining room as fast as my legs would carry me. The elegant room was very lovely, draped with huge curtains. The hand-woven rug covered the entire wooden floor. Centered precisely was a wooded oak table with matching chairs and a beautiful crystal chandelier. I walked through the door of the dining room facing my Paps at the far end of the table. On his left was Mama and his right was Sarah. Next to Sarah was Charles, and next to Mama was Joseph.

On the other end of the table was Grandma. Ann and Lily were putting the dishes on the table, and Paps and Charles were talking about the farm. Mama was telling Lily how the silverware needed a third coat of polishing. Joseph was trying to tell Grandma how he was the best warrior in the world, and as I shut the door behind me, the voices grew quiet and all eyes turned in my direction. The first to speak was Mama. She was very beautiful if you didn't know her, because her attitude turned her sour and unattractive, which it does to many. She had long hair like mine though hers was a couple of shades darker.

Her skin was the color of milk, and her eyes were the shade of the sky.

"Isabel," she said in a firm voice that would give anyone goose bumps.

"Yes'm," I was prepared for a sermon.

"Why must I ask you repeatedly to be at dinner for half-past noon every single day and still you never listen to me? Answer me that."

"Miss Laura doesn't leave until half-past noon," I said slowly and assuringly so I would speak in proper form.

"Well, that means that you would be here at exactly on time, and not making us wait. You are late, and that makes us have to wait for you, young lady!" She said raising her voice.

"Yes Mam, I understand that except I wanted to look nice for dinner so I had to change into a dress and…."

"Stop there. You need no excuses because I see that you are wearing the same dress that you were wearing for breakfast. I do not want another word out of you unless you are spoken to child. Now take your seat.

"Yes Mam." There was no use explaining that I changed after breakfast. Mama would just get madder for talking back.

I could hear Joseph telling Mama, "but she wasn't spoken to when she said that."

He was carrying on and on like that, but no one told him to behave. He was just too cute. I don't see why he bothered me so. It seemed to me that he was carrying on because he knew how it annoyed me. I guess that's how it is with a little brother.

"I certainly hope that the dinner isn't too cold since we had to wait on Isabel so long," Grandma said in a sarcastic voice that mad me feel stupid.

"Lily, Lily, the dinner is not cold is it? Well is it?" Mama asked in a frustrated tone.

"No Mistress, no Ma'm. It… it's just purfect," Lily said.

"Well, then bring it out so we can enjoy this perfect meal," Mama said and gave a look to Lily and Ann to get the dinner on the table instantly. It's funny how you can tell what someone wants just by their eyes. Someone can look at you and you know that they are either jealous or they feel sorry for you or maybe they're mad. Eyes do a lot.

"Bernice, sweety you alright?" My Paps asked addressing my Mama. My Paps had a deep voice, but it wasn't strong. He was of medium height and had chocolate brown eyes and light dusty brown hair.

"Fine Daniel, just a bit aggravated" And Mama's eyes gave me a look that told me she was angry with me.

"Calm down, think you've been just a little jangled." Paps said making sure he didn't sound too firm.

Within the next minute, Ann and Lily came out with our dinner on the china plates that were in our family for a great deal of time. Mama said that they were more important than some people.

"Finally!" Grandma said in a snooty voice.

"So sorry, Mistress. Sorry." Ann and Lily said simultaneously. I guess they were used to having to apologize for themselves.

Ann and Lily opened the cover on the plates so we could see what we were having. As they pulled off the cover, I could see the steam crawling out trying to set itself free. When the platters were fully opened, I could see what we were having. To my recollection we had baked ham, steamed corn, beets, mashed potatoes, and fresh baked rolls. It was one of my favorite meals.

I heard Mama say, "Lordy, ham again." She said it in a voice like, why are we having ham when we had it three days ago. The food went around the table so everyone could pick out what they wanted and how much. Grandma started talking about the baby, Sarah's baby... if she wanted a boy or a girl and so on.

"I do hope it is a little girl. I really do want a girl," Sarah said in a hopeful voice.

"Oh yes, a little girl would be lovely," Mama said.

"Well, Charles how about you, what are you hoping for? Paps asked.

"Oh, I don't care as long as Sarah's happy." Charles responded.

"You got yourself a fine man Sarah, a fine man." Grandma said in a voice like I'm happy for you, and I wish I had someone like that.

"Thank you Mrs. Hamilton, that was very nice of you to say." Charles said blush-ing, but you could tell he was charmed.

Without thinking I said, "Sarah what month is the baby going to come?"

Before Sarah could answer my question Mama said, "What did I tell you earlier about not talking unless you are spoken to! Are you deliberately disobeying me?"

"No Ma'm," I just wasn't thinking. "I'm sorry."

"You should be sorry. Now Isabel, I don't want this to happen again child. Do I make myself clear?" Her tone was so shrill that it wouldn't surprise me none if it would break glass.

"Yes'm," I said.

I turned to look at Paps and he was just nodding his head not saying a word. It seemed like he never would set his own opinions on some matters. He would just do what everyone else was doing. My Paps was a follower, as I said earlier. That goes total opposite for my Mama. Boy, she would set her own rules and do what she wanted. She would never follow anyone else even if she agreed with them. People would surely follow her though, Paps mostly. Whatever she said he would just nod his head, even if he didn't agree. Of course, you never knew if he agreed or not because he would never say anything. I guess it was pretty obvious who was boss of our family.

When Paps was finished with his dinner, he left because he had to go into town to the bank.

"I'll be back around three. I shouldn't be any longer than that. Charles, go and help out Matthew and Phillip outside. Oh, and tell Phillip that he can leave early today."

"No problem," Charles said nodding his head.

"Oh Papa, can I come with you?" Joseph whined.

"If you came with me who would I get to watch over all the ladies?" Paps tickled Joseph's belly making him laugh so he would forget about the bank.

"Yes, I'll stay and watch all da ladies." Joseph said acting like he had this important job to do.

"That's a boy, Joseph!" Paps walked out of the dining room. Minutes later Charles left to go head out to the fields to follow Pap's orders.

My Grandma turned to Sarah and said, "Sarah let's go and finish the bonnet and booties we were crocheting for the baby. In fact, Bernice you can start on a dress."

"What if it's a boy? A boy can't wear no dress," Joseph retorted which made Mama and Grandma laugh at such a speech.

"All babies wear dresses…boys or girls," Grandma said still laughing a bit.

"I knew that," Joseph said acting like he was just too cute for words. I wanted to tell him to stop acting like he was three. I mean he was six years old. They all went into the living room while I was still in the dining room. Soon Lily and Ann were clearing away the dishes from the table, and I was still sitting in the same chair admiring the flowers that stood inside the vase in the center of the table. It didn't bother me that no one noticed I was still sitting there. Wull, maybe I cared…

I made sure to tell Lily and Ann thanks for the dinner as I left the room. I always tried to say thanks because I knew how important it was to hear that word. When you put hard work or effort into something its always seems worthwhile when someone thanks you for it. So I always tried my best to say it at the right time. Lily knew I must of been feeling kinda of bad because she patted my head and told me to go on outside to get some fresh air. I agreed and walked through the kitchen door instead of going through the living room. I didn't want to hear a sly remark either by Mama or Grandma.

Chapter 6

I walked on outside and took a deep breath and let all the freshness of the air into my body. It felt good, so refreshing. I walked forward and let the sun's rays beam on-to my back. While I was walking, I allowed all the dirt to go through my toes by squishing them in the ground. I could smell the spring rising through the flowers. I skipped over to one of the five benches which were directly in the middle of the slave cabins. There were about ten cabins on either sides of the benches. I stood on the top of one of the benches and reached to the tree which was covered with red delicious apples. I grabbed the juiciest one I saw. It was ripe and ready to eat.

I figured Emma was already in the cotton field working, but I went to check her cabin anyway. She shared it with two other women, but I only knew them by name. I knocked once then opened the door and saw that the cabin was empty. There was no way the cabin could have been big enough for three people. It was a small ole thing. There were three little cots stuffed into the corner, and a couple of hooks where they hung their dresses. I knew that Martha had three dresses but I didn't know how many the other two woman had. I shut the door, and there stood Ole Uncle.

"Hey, Ole Uncle! How ya' doin'?" I totally forgot about my proper way of speaking when I was outside because I knew no one would mind out there. It was like a totally different world, and it was just outside of my house.

"Wull, hey Miss Izzy. I'm doin' mighty fine. How 'bout yerself?" Ole Uncle said in his deep southern voice. Why I never heard such a deep voice. He was carrying a heavy load of lumber on his shoulder, and he was sure sweating bullets. He was a big, tall ole man. He had a full head of gray hair and beard too. His only means of family were sold. I think one of them ended up with the Brownson's. They were considered our neighbors although they lived a good twenty miles away.

I finally answered Ole Uncle's question. I was just daydreaming away once again. I could see that he was waiting for me to respond, "Oh, I'm doin' pretty good. I mean I've had better days if you know what I mean."

"I knows whatcha mean. I've hads plenty of dose days. Now Izzy, if I's don'ts gets a goin' on my way I's think I'll just break down with this here heavy load." Ole Uncle said with his huge smile. Why he was smiling from ear to ear. I swore I could see every one of his teeth.

"Oh, alright Ole Uncle I'll be seeing you, and try not to let that load break you down," I said smiling back.

"I's do my bests. See ya around Miss Izzy." And Ole Uncle was on his way.

I decided that I was gonna head to the cornfields because it was a heck of a lot closer than the cotton fields, and I knew that Jones would be in the cornfields, so I thought I would visit with him. I saw that Phillip, one of Paps helpers, was by the cornfields making sure everybody was working. He was a short and chubby man. He must of smoked tobacco weed every chance he got because I remember always smelling him from a mile away. Talk about bad teeth, every single one of them was yellow or brown. I even think he was missing a few. He was just the dirtiest thing you ever saw.

"Isabel, whatcha doing o'er here?" Phillip asked me. I told him I was taking the short cut to the river to feed the ducks. I made sure that I was out of sight before I turned abrubtly to the cornfield on the left. I ran through the short stalks with my arms spread out like I was flying. It was so peaceful. Nothing could go wrong. There were no worries when I flew. Gliding through the field, I bumped into Ticey who was working away. She had a set of the biggest brown eyes. She must of been around Sarah's age at that time. She was working pretty hard when I saw her cause I remember the sweat was running off her body so fast you could of sworn she just jumped into a lake or something.

"Izzy, whatcha doin' guh?" Ticey asked as she burst into tears.

"Ticey, what's wrong. You all right?" I tried to comfort her.

"Oh Izzy, it's jus' horrible." She could hardly talk; she was crying so hard.

"What is it? What happened?" Even though I asked her I didn't want to find out. Do you ever feel like that when you have to ask because you need to find out, but you really don't want to because you know it's gonna hurt.

Ticey was taking deep breaths so she could tell me what the terrible thing was that was making her cry so. "Junior gettin' sold ups in Macon tomo'row. That's whats they tolds me 'n Cranby." Her tears poured out like a waterfall. I didn't know what to say. I mean what do you tell a person who has just found out she might not see her own child ever again—I'm sorry, too bad— Sorry has lost basically all its meaning because people say it just too much. Junior was only about four years old. What would he do without his Mama and Papa?

I had to say something, "Ticey I am truly sorry. I can't believe this happened. I mean I don't know why Paps would do something like this to ya'll." I was flabbergasted.

"It ain't yer fault. Don't go and gets yerself self inta trouble which a Papa now, ya hear."

I nodded. "How's Cranby taking it?" I asked her 'cause I knew that sometimes Cranby let his anger take over him. He had scars to prove that.

"Cranby mad as hell. I hopes he don't do nothin' stupid ta gets himself killed." I could see Ticey's hope was being destroyed; it was being crushed into a little ball. It was like she was being eaten alive. "I's might never sees my baby evers again, my little angel." She was so hurt and heart-broken. There was nothing that I could say that would make her feel any better.

"Don't you believe that Ticey. You will see him again only if you believe that you will. You gotta have faith because if you have faith then you will see the miracles happen right before your eyes." I think I was echoing Emma's words to me. I like to think that we can trade words with each other in times of trouble. Looking directly in those big brown eyes of hers, I told

Ticey never to give up hope. Staring right into someone's eyes brings more meaning to the words, at least that's what Miss Laura always said.

I gave ger a hug so tight because I could tell she needed one. I told her I should go because Phillip was pretty close by; I knew this because I could smell him. She knew it, too. I walked away just thinking about Ticey, Cranby, and Junior. I felt so terribly bad for what they must go through. I should of been crying, but I never used to cry. I put everything behind me and tried not to worry about it. I would swallow up all the pain that was there.

I ran over to Matthew, another one of Paps helpers, and I was going to ask him about Junior. He was a little bit nicer than Phillip but not much.

"Matthew, Matthew!!!" I yelled so he'd turn around.

"Whatcha want Isabel?" He responded in a very uninterested way.

"Matthew why we selling Junior. He's a good boy, ain't done nothing wrong before. He never caused any trouble."

"Listen girly, that ain't none of your damn business. You stay out of that. Now go along." Matthew said in a very disturbed and angry way. He was trying to scare me away, but he didn't frightened me any.

"But I..."

"But nothing. Keep still, Isabel!"

I didn't speak another word to him. Not because he scared me any but because there was obviously nothing I could say that would change his mind or help any. I would just get myself yelled at. Not that being yelled at bothered me, but I just found it a complete waste of time really.

"Oh shoot!" I said as I was walking away.

Chapter 7

I was dying of thirst so I decided to walk over to the water well. I poured the ladle into the water and got me about two cupfuls. I thought that I deserved to sit down to enjoy a nice cup of cold water to give a final push of pain that was still in my throat. Shading my eyes from the glare in the sun, I saw Emma trudging down the path to the well. She must of been thirsty, too. When she reached the well, she was like a tired dog, lapping up water. I looked down at her hands and got the chills because you know how I told you she worked in the cotton field, well she always was cutting up her hands on those darn prickers. Her hands were always pretty blistered up and bleeding. It wasn't a pretty sight. She always worked in the cotton field since I can remember. In fact, one time Phillip thought she wasn't working hard enough or something so right then and there he pulled up her dress and beat her. That wasn't the only time she had gotten beat though. No one really counted because everyone pretty much got beat a lot. Lordy, if you only heard some of the stories Emma and Jones would tell, your mouth wouldn't shut for a week, and I can put money behind that, too.

"What's the matter guh? You forgots how ta talk," Emma said just joking around with me because I was just standing there in a daze.

"Hey Emma," I said wearing a big grin. If you haven't noticed it didn't take much to make me smile or laugh. Emma said I should always keep it quality. I made sure I did.

"That's mo'e like its," Emma said as we both laughed.

"I guess you heard 'bout Junior?" I asked her.

"Guh, I's was da one who tolds Ticey. Ya know thats I'm always findin' outs 'bout stuff likes dis." Emma said.

"Yeah, it's sad, isn't Emma." I took another sip of my water. "Hell, lifes sad Izzy. Least he's still goin' be alives. That's happens ta me plenty of times. Likes I saids befo'e, it's hard when ya gets attached ta.something because when it's gone…" Emma wanted me to finish what she was saying.

"It's hell." I giggled as I said that because it was the first time I said that word. Just wasn't lady like then.

"That's right, it's hell! You know Ticey could be hopin' and prayin' for that boy of hers not ta gets sold, but he's goin' be gone come tomo'row." That's the way Emma had to live, take what you get when it comes but no tears when it's gone. Emma said it how it was. Emma might have seemed harsh, but she had a very tough life to live. She sure did teach me a lot about life and about how you got to live in this world. She had a bunch of faith in God, and a lot of slaves didn't believe in God because no one taught them. Some slaves were into, I believe it was voodoo and other things such as that. Emma would try to change some people's beliefs and turn them to the Almighty. I forgot who taught Emma about God, but I know when she learned about Him she never stopped believing. I always told Emma and Jones about the Bible verses and stories I would learn from Miss Laura or at church because they always enjoyed when I taught them things because they didn't have anyone else to teach them.

"Ya can't gets sad if the sun don't shine yer way." Emma said.

"I know because if you cry every time something isn't right you will buckle up in-to nothing. And then you'll start feeling sorry for yourself." I said that and thought about Sarah who cried every time something went wrong.

Phillip was heading our way, and I knew he was getting angry seeing me and Emma talking because he yelled at her to get up, "Emma get yer big ass off that bench and get yer chores done."

"Yes sir, but I's was just gettin' some water ya see," Emma said. She always had to get her two cents in.

"Nigger breaks over," Phillip said in a very perturbed manner.

"Izzy, ya comes back lata and we talks some mo'e," Emma whispered to me as she slowly got up. She was definitely taking her time getting up.

"Nigger, you take any longer and I'll beat you on that damn table." Phillip said as he took a huge spit of his tobacco. It was disgusting.

"Ya'sir," Emma said as she got herself to the cotton field as quick as she could walking.

"What da hell were ya'll two talking 'bout?" Phillip asked as he took another spit of tobacco.

"Nothing," I said. I guess you could say I was being a little smart.

Before Phillip could say anything else to me Charles interrupted us. "Phillip, hey cowboy, you can leave early today. Go on home to your wife you crazy bastard!" Charles yelled from Lady, his big golden brown horse. I guess Charles didn't see me standing there, or he would never have said that.

"See ya tomorrow," Phillip said taking another long look at me as he sniffed back and let out a huge spit of tobacco, once again. He kept staring at me so I did the same thing back. I looked into his eyes and tried to see who he was. I could always do that to people. I learned that from Jones. He always said the eyes are the tell of a person. When I looked into Phillip's eyes I saw some sort of fear or pain of some sort. I thought maybe it was from his past, like his childhood. It didn't surprise me any because I knew a lot of people like Phillip; they had to act all mean and tough on the outside to hide their painful past. I watched him leave, and once I saw he was out of sight I jumped off the bench just missing one of Phillip's big spit gulps. I was on my way to the cornfields skipping the entire way there.

Chapter 8

When I reached the cornfield, I went directly to me and Jones's spot. The little open square in the middle of the cornfield was ours and no one could take that from us. Me and Jones called it our special spot. It meant a great deal to both, me and Jones. It was where we had our long talks, maybe just us sitting there enjoy each others presence, or maybe staring into the big blue sky. No one ever saw us at the special spot or any-wheres elses I guess. I just don't think anyone cared about my comings and goings in those days.

Jones spotted me walking towards him. "Is thats you Izzy? I's was beginin' ta won'er when ya was comin' visit me."

"Come on, Jones, let's go sit." Jones knew I just felt like talking. He wasn't scared of getting into trouble for not working because for one thing it was the beginning summer and the corn stalks were still a bit low, and we were in the direct center of the field. Also, I knew that Phillip had left, and I knew Jones wanted a break just by looking at his face. His face was so tired and worn out.

No telling why me and Jones chose this spot to be our special one, but we did. It was all ours. This probably sounds silly now, but we called it our little heaven because it was perfect to us and nothing could go wrong there. When we reached it, it was like as if we felt safe. We laid down and stared at the clouds. We would try to make images out of them. Some of them would look like dogs, cats and others would look like houses or certain people.

Jones must of known what I was thinking because he sat up. I knew he was gonna say something so I turned my head and looked at him.

"Ya know worse thangs are gonna happens than Junior gettin' sold. Shore its sads ta see him goin', but slaves been killed on dis here plantation." I turned my face away because my throat burned, you know that feeling when you could cry but you don't. I swallowed it up like every other time I thought I could cry.

When I looked back at him he was staring up in the clouds again. "Jones?"

"Yeah, Izzy."

"Was it always this bad? I mean was there always killing?"

Since I can remember Izzy. Theys always been killin' of slaves since it all started. The mo'e pow'rful someones thinks they is da mo'e they use it." He looked back at me. "Izzy when peoples thinks that's they are pow'rful then theys starts ta think they don't need nobody. Whens they thinks that, that's when theys go wrong. Izzy, yous taught me ta puts God first, and whens peoples thinks that they in mo'e control than God then they ain't puttin' God first now ares they. You knows who taught me all 'bout that?"

I nodded.

"Yous dids Izzy. So I tries ta do it because I's knows yer a sma't guh." Jones said.

"Jones, do you ever feel like leaving all this hatred and just running away? You could be free from all problems. I just want to go away sometimes and live a new life where there is no hatred. You know." I looked at him and now his face was away from the clouds and now completely on me.

"Izzy, shore that sounds great. A new life withouts hate, but Izzy ya knows there ain't such a place. You's can't just runs away from yer pro'lems. Why, hell if so, just 'bout every slave from every parts would be gone."

"Why don't ya'll runaway. Ya'll have to live this life of slavery when ya'll could be free." I put a piece of corn straw in my mouth.

"Cause yous can't runs away from e'erything yous don't like. You gots ta face yer pro'lems, whatever theys may be. Plus, I'm betters than thats. I ain't no fool. Izzy, I wakes up e'rey morin' befo'e sunrise and I's works for nothing because I'm a slave, a colored man. I wakes ups sometimes sick as a dog, and I's don't wanna gets up. But Izzy, I do cause if I's didn't the

29

white man would punish me. Ya don't think that I never thinks 'bout running' away? Shore I do, but I gets back ta my senses. I knows I'm better than that. I get sick of being trapped, Izzy. Sometimes I just wanna breaks free, but I gotta live with da life God gave me. I thinks he chose 'specially for me."

I was speechless. I had no idea what to say. I just remember going to him and hugging him and him hugging me back.

After that, we just talked about silly things–nothing too serious. I remember all of a sudden the extremely hot sun was covered up by monstrous gray clouds like a snap of the fingers. As the clouds grew darker, the water drops began to fall. How fast the beautiful day turned to gray.

At that time, I was telling Jones a passage that I read in the Bible about faith. About faith in God and how faith will bring you to God, to eternity. As I was finishing it up, it began to pour. I mean the rain was coming out like buckets. Jones and I watched everybody run to shelter to get out of the rain. They were afraid of getting a little wet, but not me and Jones we stayed. Jones and I loved the rain while everyone else was hiding from it. We watched Charles and Matthew go inside to escape the rain so the coast was clear. Jones and I stood up and leaned our heads back, getting all the purity from the water. We laughed as we tried to swallow the big clear drops. We started dancing like little children did. I remember thinking that me and Jones were five again. We were certainly acting that way. We twirled in the rain like tulips blooming in a garden. Jones and I looked at one another, laughed and grabbed each others hands and ran. We ran like swift leopards in a jungle. As the rain grew heavier, our speed increased. We didn't let go of our hands the entire time. Our hair was soaking; and our clothes were drenched, but we didn't care. We weren't thinking of who we were. It wasn't an elderly male slave and a young white Miss running through the field; it was two best friends and that is how we saw it. We were having the greatest time. When I was running, I wasn't thinking about anything; my mind was clear. I didn't ask Jones but I could tell he was clear in mind, too. The smile on his face was of a crescent moon. I could tell he didn't have a worry in the world. When we ran, we would fly like two birds soaring through the sky. When we flew nothing in the world could stop us; we were too forceful. We had no limits except for the sky. Our eyes got so big when we flew; they were the size of big ripe Georgia peaches.

Me and Jones ran until the rain stopped. Soon as it did Jones smiled at me with eyes of comfort. We were as wet as ever though, but we were still laughing away like two little children having a tea party. We walked slowly back to our special spot, and Jones picked up his hoe and started working once again. I left, seeing that he needed to get back to work.

Chapter 9

I saw that Matthew and Charles had come back on their horses getting everybody back to work as I made my way to the old oak. To reach the old oak you had to go through the cotton field. I was walking through the field with the small shrubs of prickers and white balls of cotton on the ends rubbing against my feet; I saw cute little Junior plucking at the cotton as fast as he could. His poor finger tips were bleeding from missing the cotton and getting the thorns caught in his soft, tender skin. Any white child his age would be crying for their mother, but slaves were to be raised tough. I walked up to him, and he was grinning away not even thinking about the deep cuts that sliced his hands.

"Hey Junior. How are you doing?" I asked him as I tapped his head. My voice grew weak. "Hey Izzy. I'm down' good," He said looking at me with his lemon-shaped, deep brown eyes which had so much happiness and youth in them.

"You probably won't understand this now but I'm telling you anyway. Junior, you have to remember to be strong. It ain't going to be easy, but no matter what you gotta keep your strength. Alright, be **strong**." I told him that emphasizing the word strong.

He looked at me again and said, "Be strong." He said with a lisp. I kissed his forehead, and I was back on my way to the old oak. I knew he was already as strong as they come at that age, but I had to tell him anyway.

When I finally reached the monstruous old oak, I took a seat on one of her stumps. Her arms comforted me as I leaned against her trunk. I sat there remembering a time when Jones and I sat in that very spot where he taught me a valuable lesson that I kept with me my whole life.

Since I was born and raised on a plantation, I never knew it was wrong to have slaves. I liked some of them, but I never really thought of them as anything else. I was blind until Jones opened my eyes for the first time and he let me see the light. He was telling me about some slave that got beaten for not working hard enough, and I told him that whites were supposed to do that when a slave did something wrong. I told him whites were better than slaves, more important. I never forgot the words Jones said after I said that disgusting statement. Jones's words always would really stick like glue.

He told me this word for word as I remember it. "Izzy, this ain't right makin' all Negroes do whats the white man say. Thats ain't right. Yous can do whate'er ya likes. I cans only do whats the white man says. O'er here I ain't even considered a man. I's considered a nigger with no feelin's or cares. Tell me da difference between ya Paps and me. The onlys thang that's different is he white and I colored. Even though he lives different thans me that don't makes him anymo'e of a man thans me. I believe that's I's a man. And no one can takes that from me. I mights not die free, but I's gonna die a man. I breathe da same air as ya Paps does. Ya knows whats it's like ta be treated likes an animal. Gettin' sold when theys don't wantcha no mo'e. Gettin' sold from ya family or gettin' beat when ya done some'pin' wrong. Wull, it shore is hell, hurts mo'e than cuttin' ya knee. I tell ya that much. Izzy, I hates to say dis ta ya, but ya need ta know dis now and when ya grows older. Yous shouldn't be complainin' with whats ya got cause if ya gots some'pin' ta complain about you gots too much. Ya gots ta be thankfuls with whatcha gots. Izzy, it shouldn't be like dis. Instead of fightin' we should join sides."

I never let those words escape me as long as I lived. Those words changed my life forever. He changed my perception of things. He opened my eyes. That's when I made a promise to myself that I would never cry again for the rest of my life because if I had anything to cry about it wasn't as half as bad as what others didn't cry about. I then learned that slavery was wrong, and just because I grew up one way didn't mean it was right. Whoever taught you to hate was wrong. No matter what a person does to you, you can't hate them. You can hate what they are doing, but you can't hate one of God's sons or daughters.

You have to give people a chance because chances are, you will like a part of them and see a part of you in them. I was raised to hate slaves because whites were supposedly more important. I soon learned that all people were equal, blacks, whites we are all the same on the inside. We are all made from the same God.

I moved from the old oak's trunk and climbed up to one of her long thick arms. I crawled to the end of it to get enough sun to dry my damp clothes from the rain. When I reached my destination, I laid on my stomach so I had a perfect view of the plantation. Wull, except I couldn't see the cane field. In Albany, where we lived planters were usually just used to having one major field on a plantation. That's one thing that made the Wadsworth Estates so special; we had three major fields. That's one reason we had so many more slaves than the other planters in Albany. We had triple the land than other plantations. Albany wasn't a real big town compared to some places in Georgia, but I remember people from other towns coming to see our plantation. Why, I remember some folks came up from Savannah to see our place. No one could believe that Paps got a cane field in Albany. Georgia wasn't much for cane fields, and people couldn't believe that we had one. People had to see with their own eyes.

When I was all dried up I made it back to the front porch and was about to open the front door, but I turned around to face the land instead. I tell you from the front porch looking out, it was beautiful. It was like a picture you would find in a book. I stared out past the horizon as far as my eyes could take me. I looked up at the sun and raised my arms. I took a deep breath and thought about the day. I thought about how I was really living in this world, and this was my life. Did that ever happen to you, you stop and think—Lordy, this is the life I was given?

I looked inside the window right next to the two doors that open to the foyer, and there they were— the three ladies, Grandma, Mama, and Sarah sipping their tea. I was surprised to see that Mrs. Brownson wasn't over. It seemed like every time they had tea Mrs. Brownson and her daughter were over too.

They were both real genuine people. I'm sure Mama never knew that though. Mama only liked to have them over because they might not of been as pretty and thin as she was. Mama always had to be the prettiest in a room, that's why she liked to have Mrs. Brownson and her daughter over for tea so much. Mama may have been prettier than Mrs. Brownson if you didn't know either one of them, but if you got to know them you would definitely think Mrs. Brownson was prettier. She had such a beautiful personality. Boy, could she cook too. There was hardly any white woman who would cook anything in those days—at where we lived—but I can remember eating her crumpets and her cookies. They were so good; they were really something to talk about.

I decided not to go through the doors because I figured I would get into some kind of trouble. I knew I had to be pretty dirty because of the rain and all. I bet they would of said something like how I was sixteen, and I acted like I was five or six. It was true though I didn't do what the average sixteen year old did then. I didn't drink tea in the afternoon. Nor other hours of the day, and I didn't know how to croquet or knit anything. I was lousy at carrying on "women" conversations. They didn't interest me much. I know that's wrong because Miss Laura always told me that one should find interest in every topic, but I think at that age I was just a little more into adventurous things.

Chapter 10

I walked around the house to go through the kitchen entrance instead. I saw that Lily and Ann were preparing supper. Mmm, mmm, it smelled delicious. I could taste the corn steaming in the boiling water. Ann turned around as she heard the door open.

"Hey guh! Where has ya been alls day?" Ann said as she poured the rice into the pot. The steam from the pot filled the small room.

"Outside I guess," I said shrugging my shoulders.

"Yous been out this whole time. Guh, it's almost supper time," Ann said.

"I know, time just slipped away," I said

I looked at Lily and she was stirring something in a pot. I don't remember what she was stirring; all I remember is how good it smelled. She hadn't said anything yet, but as she wiped her hands on her apron, she turned at me and squealed in her high voice.

"Izzy look yea self! Yous a mess. Yer dress, yer hair!!" She squealed, "Lets me see yer hands." I showed them to her. "Oh my goodness. You's a mess if I evers saw ones," she shrieked, "Ann watch alls the food while I goes clean this child up," Lily said referring to me. I didn't know why Ann never said anything about my appearance. I guess she didn't notice, but I don't know how she couldn't notice. Lily ran me up the stairs so fast I was positive that no one saw either of us. We went to my bedroom, and she grabbed the rag and dipped it in the ivory crescent bowl and started washing the dirt off my face.

"I ain't ever gonna be dones in time with ya. Izzy I's gonna fill da tub in da washroom up with some warm water. So you's can wash youself up." As she was saying this, she was nodding making sure I understood.

"Alright." I responded cheerfully.

Lily ran out the room to go and get started on the tub. I sat down in the chair facing the mirror. I always looked in the mirror to see what I was, what I was made of. I would try to read myself. I was so good at reading others I didn't understand why I couldn't read myself. I could tell what people were like by just looking into their eyes, but when I looked into mine I never saw anything. I could never see what my strengths were. I stared in the mirror trying as hard as I could, but I couldn't see anything, nothing. I would get aggravated because I would try so hard to see something. I kept pushing for me to see something. While I kept trying, I was soon interrupted by the sound of sweet Lily's voice.

"Come on Izzy the tub's all ready for ya." We hurriedly walked to the wash room.

"Now, Izzy ya don'ts take too long now, ya hear." Lily said as she shut the door behind her.

I got into the tub and allowed the warm water to crawl inside my pores. I could have fallen asleep because it was relaxing. I would have stayed inside the tub for hours, but I knew I didn't have a whole lot of time left so I hurried up and finished. I got into a suitable enough dress for supper, and I had just began to comb my hair when Lily came in.

"I'll be down in a second," I said while giving one last stroke of the brush down my long hair.

Lily nodded and walked out of the room. I could hear her saying, "What's am I's gonna do with that's girl," all the way down the stairs.

As I walked down the steep wooden staircase, I felt like the steps were growing larger as I was shrinking in them and then I was soon nothing. I had to overcome that. When I finally reached the dinning room, I was just thinking about "what if's." I was thinking like what if I could do this or what if I could do that. Then I remembered the time I was telling Jones my what if's, and his response was, "that it's great to say you're gonna to do certain things but you gotta stop just saying it. You really gotta to do them." He told me that you can't live your whole life on "what if's." Jones said you have to take that leap and do the impossible. Take the risk and make your dream come true. He also told me the leap may be big, but nothing has stopped me before. So my motto was always if you want anything bad enough and you believe in yourself anything is possible.

Chapter 11

I just sat properly in my chair waiting for the rest of my family to come in for supper. I sat there like a bump on the log not even offering help to Lily and Ann. They were setting the table, placing the china, that Mama thought was so important, onto the table. I could of least offered help even if they said they didn't need any. I suppose I was just too tired for words. There I go again making excuses for myself. Emma always said there is no need to make excuses for anything because soon your whole life will be made of them, and then you won't even be able to get yourself out of bed.

I watched the members of my family enter the dining room one by one. My Mama was the first one in, and she took her seat surprised to see I was already seated. Joseph was in after my Grandma, and Paps soon followed Sarah and Charles in. No one spoke; we just sat and waited to be served. The silence grew, and I don't know why but for some reason the silence bothered me.

I guess as it did Charles for he was the first to break it, "How many slaves did you get from Dawson?" Charles directed to my Paps. I'm sure he really didn't care about that—he just wanted to break the silence.

"I only got two," Paps said with frustration.

Grandma interrupted them, "Boys, boys do we really need to hear about this at supper?" She said slowly and in the most dignified way.

"Sorry about that, Ma'm," Charles said a little embarrassed.

"No need to be sorry. It is quite alright. I just think we can find a better conversation topic for supper." Again in the same slow and dignified voice.

"She's right," Paps said and before he could say anything else the food was being served.

The rest of the evening wasn't much of a change. The conversations were dull, and the time went by slowly. I don't think I opened my mouth once the entire time at supper, except to place the food in my mouth. Soon everyone was finished with their meal and were all leaving the dinner table. After all the chairs were empty, I made my way out thanking Lily and Ann for supper.

When I got to my bedroom, I got out my journal and began to write. The journal was a small and rectangular book made from an oak tree. Wull, at least that is what the lady said at the store. I remember Mr. Brownson had given me some money for helping him out with something. I forgot what I helped him with, but it was silly. Not silly, but nothing worth paying someone for it. I rode into town and bought the first thing I saw that I liked. Not the smartest thing to do, but I never had money before so I didn't know what I was doing.

Inside the journal I wrote down my dreams, ambitions, my goals, and my fears. I just wrote as the thoughts came to me. I could just sit and write forever. That night I wrote until I ran out of paper, and I didn't have enough energy to go down stairs to the library to get more. Instead, I made myself start reading the Odyssey, the book Miss Laura gave me to read. I remember opening the book and smelling the adventure that lay within the pages. Reading the first page, I immediately became a part of the story. The story was about a man, Odysseus, who had to go and fight in the Trojan War, and the journeys in order for him to get home were amazing. It took him twenty years to finally get home: ten because of the Trojan War and another ten years because of all the wild creatures, odd lands, gods, and goddesses he ran into. While I read the story, I pretended that it was me who had to get home from the Trojan War. When I read, I felt as if it was me who wanted to kill Troy and that it was really me on all the adventures.

Before I got to bed that night, Odysseus had already fought the Trojans and having won the war, he was on his way home. He ran into his first adventure which was the "land of the Lotus Eaters." You see, if you ate the lotus you became addicted to it.

The lotus made you not want to leave or get up from where you were. A loss of hope was upon you as if you were worthless.

I was falling asleep after the "land of the Lotus Eaters" and right as I shut my eyes I heard a slow squeak of the door opening, and I knew that it was Lily. She was tip-toeing to make sure she wouldn't wake me up.

"You don't have to keep quiet. I'm already awake."

"Oh, I didn't wakes ya Izzy, did I's?" Lily asked me in a worried voice.

"No, I was up."

"Good, I's would have felt right bad," She said as she pulled up the covers over my shoulders and up to my neck just the way I liked it.

"Good nights Izzy and haves a good, nice dream," Lily said.

"You too, Lily." She rubbed my forehead and then left the room.

Chapter 12

I slept dreamless that night. I felt like I had been sleeping for days when Lily woke me up Thursday morning. Even though I had gotten plenty of rest I was somewhat tired.

"Izzy wakes up, guh," Lily said in a scratchy whisper.

I shook my head several times and said, "Alright, I'm up, I'm up." I raised my arms above my head and stretched while breathing morning air.

"Good Izzy, now get dressed. I'll be backs in a bits to see if yous dressed."

I nodded my head. I lay in my bed for another minute thinking about how days went by so swiftly and soon this one would be over, too. I thought that I should make the best of it, but I hadn't a clue how. I sat up with my feet hanging off to the side the bed swinging my legs and rubbing my eyes with my hands. I walked over to the bowl that Lily had just filled up with cold water. I dipped my face into the bowl several times before I knew I was fully awake. I grabbed the neatly folded towel that was placed next to the bowl and dried my face. I started brushing my hair while I looked into the mirror. I tried to read myself again, and this time I tried even harder and longer than before. Disappointment visited me again for I saw nothing, nothing but a southern girl with big brown eyes and long auburn hair. For some reason I couldn't see past that; I didn't understand why. I got myself so annoyed ever time.

Breakfast that morning wasn't much different than usual. Although I think I spoke this morning. Oh yes I responded to a question with the "Yes mam." Not much of conversation, was it?

After breakfast, I drug myself to the library because I knew I should get started on some of the work Miss Laura assigned, but I really didn't want to. As I was about to start one of the assignments, I yelled out "Junior!" Oh gosh, I thought to myself. I got up, and ran straight through the front doors, passing up

Mama, Grandma, and Sarah in the living room. I was sure they probably said something about how they never saw a young lady running through a house so fast. I got outside and ran down the porch stairs and onto the grass which was still wet from the morning dew. I ran to see if they had taken Junior yet.

I ran to where I saw Cranby and Ticey. I saw that Paps was taking Junior into town to the people who were buying him. Junior was wearing a big smile on his face as Matthew lifted him up into the wagon. As the wagon was pulling away, tears welled up from Junior eyes. He realized that the wagon was pulling away from his mama and papa. I saw that Ticey was crying too and reaching out for her only baby. Cranby had to hold her back for she longed to run after the wagon. I looked back at the wagon and I saw Junior reaching for his Mama too. My throat stung as I saw the tears fall off their cheeks, and my face reddened because there was nothing I could do. As ususal, I swallowed the pain back down. Once Junior, was out of sight, Cranby let go of Ticey, and she ran off somewhere. I bet it was to the old oak. Cranby was still standing there devastated at what had just happened. Poor Cranby, poor Ticey I thought. Man, if you just looked at Cranby, you would never think that he was the type to care about anything. He had a rough face and eyes of stone. That's just one reason you shouldn't judge a person on the way they look. You would of never known how big his heart was until you met him. It kinda reminded me of what Miss Laura always told me about how you can't judge a book by it's cover. Now, I see it goes with people too.

I wanted to say something to Cranby because he was still standing there, just staring out from where the wagon pulled his baby away. I had to say something.

"Cranby, I'm gonna be honest; I haven't a clue what to say. I mean, shoot, sometimes I think I have it bad. I guess I'm just selfish, because here you lost your little boy and I might be complaining cause my toe hurts. I mean really I feel for you, honest. Sometimes I wonder what God's plan is. I wonder why He does things like this. The preacher said once everything happens for a reason, but then I think what's the reason for this. Is it some sort of warning or punishment? I sometimes wish I could see what was going on in God's mind. What are His reasons, just so I could understand them." I didn't realize I was rambling when I told Cranby that, but he didn't seem to mind.

"Yeah," He said turning his head to look at me.

"Who'd a thought this would happen." After I said that I wanted to punch myself in the stomach. It was just a stupid thing to say.

"Who's I kiddin'? I knews it was gonna hap'en. Then I's told myself it wasn't gonna. I's started ta thinks it won't hap'en ta me. Who's I kiddin'? I mean right when I said it wasn't gonna hap'en ta Junior is rights when it did. It hap'ens ta us all," Cranby said barely finishing his sentences.

Cranby's eyes met mine and they locked; a tear rolled down his cheek. I fought for words to say and I couldn't say any or I didn't know how. I felt that if I spoke, then I would just bust into tears.

"Cranby get yer self back to work now! Today's nothing special!" Phillip yelled from his horse. I wanted to go and hit Phillip so hard that he wouldn't know what happened to him. Cranby nodded. He put his hands in his pockets and started walking.

"It's all going to be different one day," I whispered to the wind as the words fell out of my mouth without me even realizing it. As Cranby was walking, he looked back at me, and then walked on through the fields.

Chapter 13

My knees were weak and my throat stung and pain filled my body, but once again I swallowed all the pain that was within me. I walked up the porch and through the doors, and there was the three ladies sitting and chatting.

"Back so soon Isabel?" My Grandma said in a snobbish expression.

I nodded and kept walking toward the library.

"Isabel, you answer your Grandmother when she speaks to you, or are you too high and mighty to answer to any of us?" My Mama said in a very stern manner with a pinch of sarcasm.

"Sorry, Mama. Grandma, I'm sorry. I felt like coming back inside and doing some of the work Miss Laura assigned to me."

"Well, then get to it," Mama said.

When I reached the library, I began to read more of the Odyssey. I got to this part where there was a Cyclops named Polyphemus. He was a huge monster with one eye. It was very difficult for me, I mean Odysseus to get out of this one. I pretended it was me who blinded the big ugly beast. I had to blind Polyphemus so he wouldn't hurt any of us.The eye judges so... I had to blind Polyphemus so he couldn't make judgemments on what he sees; he couldn't stop us from being free.

I read about Athena, goddess of wisdom and about how she was very helpful to Odysseus. The book was just growing more exciting; I could barely put the book down, but I realized that it was dinner time. Throughout the entire dinner I couldn't stop thinking about Odysseus. I couldn't wait to see what adventure I would have to go on next.

Chapter 14

I was outside on the porch rocking back and forth on the oversized, white, wooden chair that could of fit two other people. I was just daydreaming thinking about me and Jones and how one day we would be free together and fly through the fields. I stood up grabbed my white lace bonnet and hopped down the big porch steps onto the green, green grass. I was singing to myself as I often did. I didn't know too many songs by heart, so I would make them up. The songs I made up never made any sense. They were just about things I saw. I would sing although I didn't carry that much of a tune.

I walked over to the apple tree and plucked an apple of its stem. I took the first bite letting the juice fall into my mouth. The first bite of an apple is the hardest part to bite, but it is the best.

I was walking through the cornfield smelling the corn stalks—the dry yet sweet smell. I remember the corn always smelling wonderful, so deliscous. I saw that Jones was taking a break because he lying down with his arms behind his head in our special spot.

"Hey Izzy," Jones said in his warm voice.

"Hi, Jones." I joined him on the ground taking the last bite of my apple.

Me and Jones really didn't say too much after that. That's what was so special about us, we had the kind of friendship where we were happy just sitting next to one another not saying a word. Sometimes peacefulness is just as good as caring on a full conversation.

"Jones, you know how ta swim?" I asked out of the blue.

"Naw, sure don't. What 'bout yerself?" Jones asked.

"No, but I'd like to learn. I don't know it always struck me as something fun," I said.

"I's like ta learns, too. Hey, tells ya what whoever learns ta swim first ya gotta teach the other one," Jones said putting out his hand to shake for a deal. I put my hand out, and we shook on it. It was a set deal.

We both laid back down and didn't have a worry in our mind. I let the sun redden my cheeks and freckle my nose. I only had a few freckles on my nose and Jones really didn't have any, but we pretended we were covered with little freckles all over our face. We've always heard of people that were covered in freckles, and we've always wanted to meet them. All the children characters in books always had tons of freckles, and when I told that to Jones we both immediately wanted to have them, too.

"Izzy?" Jones asked me.

"Yeah, Jones?"

"Feels like flyin'?" Jones asked.

"Always, Jones, always," I said more in a whisper.

We stood up together holding hands and looking at each other. We did it. We flew through the cornfields. My hair was going wild through the wind. As our speed in-creased, so did our dreams. You see we believed that we were really flying. I still think we flew till this day. Our free hand was spread out as far as it could reach. We were zooming through the air. We soon stopped, and Jones felt he should get back to work.

As I managed my way out of the field, I saw Ole Uncle filling up some buckets of water from the well. He saw me coming his way, "Why, hey, Miss Izzy. How ya doin' this fine day?"

"I'm good. How 'bout you? You doing just as good I hope."

"I's just mighty fine." He smiled and then filled another bucket.

"That's good to hear," I said.

"Miss Izzy, you always catching me at a bad time. I have to go and gets all this water in the fields because all da workers are surely hot because the suns just blazin' today." Ole Uncle picked up his buckets and was on his way, "See ya around Miss Izzy." He yelled heading toward the cornfield.

"See ya around, Ole Uncle." I yelled right back at him.

Chapter 15

I was in one of those moods where I just felt like wandering but not to any specific place. I let the rays of the hot sun shine on my back. I kept hearing a loud and squeaky tune coming from the opposite direction from where I was walking so I drifted to the tune. When I got close enough to the tune, I knew it was Emma humming away. I decided that I was going to sneak up on her. I was trying to walk as lightly as possible and Emma still heard me, "Hey Izzy!" She exclaimed and then went right back to her humming.

"Emma, how did you hear me coming? I was walking lighter than ever."

"Ta be tru'ful I's could feels someones a walkin' ups ta me, and I's just figured whos it was. I's had dis feelin' its a be yea." Emma made sure I understood.

"Oh, that's odd."

She shrugged her shoulders, "I guess."

"Well, anyway Emma how you doing?"

"Pretty goods, pretty goods. And yerself?" She wiped the sweat coming off her forehead.

"I'm good I guess. I seem to keep thinking about when Junior got taken away. It just happened so sudden; they just took Junior away. It was hard to handle all that pain. I imagine Ticey and Cranby are still heartbroken."

"Yeah, 'magine so. Izzy, ya know how I always say there's no time for tears."

I nodded my head, so she went on.

"Ya see Izzy, living like us slaves some'ping worse prolly gonna hap'en tom'row. Ya can'ts be a cryin' everyday cause some'ping didn't go right cause being a slave things hardly ever goes right. Sure it hurts, but its always gonna hurt, Izzy. Ya see stuff is always gonna seem bad, and ya can't cry ever time ya hurtin'. I's not tellin' ya not ta cry, but I's saying you can't cry ever time ya hurtin'. There is too many reasons in dis world ta cry; ya gots ta pick da right ones." She nodded for me to understand, and I nodded. To be honest when she told me that I didn't understand right away, but I didn't let her words leave me. I grew to understand them.

Emma changed the subject completely, "Learnin' any good stuff froms dat teacha of yers."

I shook my head because I was trying to understand what she had said before she changed the subject. "What? Oh yeah, um well…"

"Spit it out, guh," Emma said.

I laughed, "Miss Laura gave me this book to read called the Odyssey. I just love it. It's about this man, Odysseus, who has to go on all these adventures in order for him to return home." I paused.

"Go on, go ons." Emma was real anxious. She always liked it when I told her about things Miss Laura taught me because she never had a chance to learn from a teacher.

"Sorry, ok where was I?" I had forgotten the last thing I said.

"The mans got all da adventures to go through before he gets home." Emma wanted me to get on with the story.

"Yes, the man Odysseus has to get back to his home, Ithaca, but he can't seem to make it home because he keeps running into bizarre lands and frightful monsters. There was this one-eyed Cyclops monster who tries to kill Odysseus, but Odysseus luckily blinds him." Emma's eyes were getting bigger and bigger. I started to imitate the Cyclops walking like a big monster and talking in a heavy deep voice. We couldn't help but laugh. She kept on picking away, and before I knew it I was picking cotton with her.

"Is there any mo' stories?" Emma asked very interested.

"Yeah, there's this one island where this lady turns all Odysseus's men into pigs." Emma started dying laughing, and she made me start laughing. Emma said that she saw a pig once when she was around ten at the plantation where she worked. I never saw a live pig at that age I was then, but I knew what one looked like because I had seen them in picture books.

49

I kept on telling her stories, and we both kept plucking. Although I wasn't going as fast Emma, my fingers started bleeding. I remember them hurting real bad just from that day. I imagine Emma and the other slaves' hands hurt real bad from everyday. I would just pick a couple and put them in Emma's satchel that she had around her shoulder. Not too much later Ole Uncle came by with water. I must of been there talking with Emma for a long time because Ole Uncle had already went all through the cane field.

"Why, Miss Izzy, I just keep runnin' inta yea.." He pointed to the bucket to see if I wanted any. I took the ladle poured it into the bucket and took a huge gulp of water.

"I's hope ya ain't passin' me up. I'm thirsty too ya know," Emma' said joking around with Ole Uncle.

"I's wasn't gonna forgets ya." He held the bucket out as she gulped down her water. Emma was sweating real hard so I dipped my hands in the bucket like a cup and scooped up water, and then I poured the water on Emma's neck. At first she squealed cause it was real cold, but then she thanked me cause it felt good. After we thanked Ole Uncle, he was on his way to give out water to the others. I told Emma I should go back inside for now, but that I would be back later. Once I started heading out I could hear that loud and squeaky humming Emma was doing. I laughed out loud.

Chapter 16

I made my way back to the front porch and opened the doors to the house. I went and sunk down into the chair in the foyer when I heard a call from the living room, "Isabel is that you?" Grandma called from the living room.

I knew if I yelled from where I was I would be in trouble for being rude, so I got myself up and went to the living room.

"Yes, Mam."

"Isabel, I want you to go play the piano right now. Oh and don't feel like you can quit when you are tired. You can quit when I say. Is this understood?" Grandma commanded.

"Yes Mam." I responded with no emotion.

"Oh yes," Mama added, "Mrs. Brownson and her daughter are going to join us for tea and cake, so please do not embarrass me." Mama nodded for me to leave the room.

"Yes Mam." I didn't know how I could possibly embarrass Mama in front of Mrs. Brownson. I enjoyed Mrs. Brownson, and I believe she enjoyed me.

I left the room walking toward where the piano was. I sat down on the bench and put my favorite piece of music down, and I began to play. I loved to play the piano. The fact that I made music was unbelievable to me. I relaxed my fingers and I let the music flow through them. I was still playing by the time Mrs. Brownson and Rachel came. Rachel was more of Sarah's age than mine. I didn't bother to go and greet them because I knew Mama would be displeased and send me right back to the piano. I always have enjoyed Mrs. Brownson's company. She was real genuine person. She meant everything she said.

I tried to play lightly so that I could hear what they were talking about. I heard Mrs. Brownson ask if it was me playing the piano, but the subject was swiftly changed after the response by Mama.

Time drifted and my fingers were throbbing; they ached terribly. I felt like going sleep in my bed. The music I played began to come out slower and softer because I could barely move my fingers. I was still playing long after Mrs. Brownson and Rachel had left. I had wished I had gotten a chance to chat with Mrs. Brownson.

My back began to ache from sitting in the same spot for so long. I kept playing. Soon I felt the hot sun that was on my back disappear. By this time my fingers and back were past aching. I wasn't thinking about making the music sound beautiful anymore. I was just thinking to get through with the notes, and then I would be able to stop. I didn't understand why I had to do this, was I being punished? Why keep me here this long? I was so confused. I began to make the songs sluggish, and I felt myself not caring anymore. I told that to Jones once, and he said no matter what task you are given, even if you don't like it, do it well. Do it with some sort of passion, put your heart in it. He told me that he always gets tired of working in the fields doing the same thing over and over, but every single day he worked in the field he did it well and with his heart. I began to think how lucky I was with the things that I thought were hard. All the slaves had it a lot worse than me. How dare I be complaining I thought to myself. Once I remember reading in the Bible and it said that at one time the Hebrews were slaves to the Egyptians. I read about some of the things that the Egyptians made them do, and the Bible said that the Egyptians were wrong for having made the Hebrews their slaves. So why would it be a good thing to have slaves now I wondered. I didn't understand how people could call themselves Christians and then treat others so cruelly. I guess I would never understand.

I heard footsteps coming. I made sure that I was sitting up straight, and I looked very proper.

"Go get ready for supper. When you are finished you can wait in the dining room," Mama said.

"Yes Mam," I said relieved that I could stop. I took my hands off the keys and placed them on my lap. I tried to stretch my fingers. Oh, how they ached! They were so weak, but I wasn't gonna be complaining about it. When she left, I got up and went directly upstairs and leaped on my bed. I just lay there for a few moments and then got ready for supper. I made sure my dress was proper and neat, and then I washed my face in my bowl to give a fresh feeling. I was fixing my hair with the two sides up when I did it again. I stared in the mirror and tried to see myself. I tried to see myself even harder than ever. "See something. See something!" I yelled out of frustration. I didn't see anything once again. What was I made of? I was beginning to believe nothing. I wasn't believing.

I was the first one in the dining room so I took out the Odyssey and began to read. I got to this part where Odysseus and his men had to make a decision to go a six-headed monster named Scylla or go to a whirlpool that swallows and vomits the sea three times a day. And right as I was going to read which one he was going to choose for him and his men, my Mama came in with Sarah. I quickly put the book under my chair before Mama got a chance to see.

Soon we were all in the dining room. There was not the stillness that was there last time. There was a lot of conversations. Paps was saying how he was going to invite the governor over for supper because he was coming down to Albany. I forgot why Paps said he was going to be in town, but he was coming. Mama was excited; in fact, she and Sarah were going to buy new dresses. Mama looked at me and said I wouldn't know what to do with a pretty new dress. I didn't mind much because it was probably true. I didn't care too much for dresses. I liked the kind that I wore but sometimes Sarah and Mama would wear real fancy dresses. Mine were plain and simple which was just fine with me. I wouldn't know what to with a real fancy dress because I always get my dresses dirty somehow or another. The family continued their excited conversation about the governor of Georgia coming to eat at the Wadsworth's.

I went upstairs after supper and got into my night things. I didn't think I would be able to write any in my journal because I was just too exhausted. I walked over to my window and raised the curtain and felt the silence of the fields. There was no more working going on outside. The workers were still awake enjoying their supper. Some were going inside their cabins to eat while others ate on the tables and benches outside. I kept staring, wishing to be eating with them. Outside on those benches no one would get mad at me if I spoke out of turn. I would just laugh and eat with them and I would fit right in. I soon closed the curtain and jumped into my bed and got under the freshly washed sheets. I could tell that they had just been washed because they smelled that of summer's grass and lemons. I lay there a moment and wondered about Junior and what he was doing... how he was adjusting to life without family. I could picture his lost eyes looking at unfamiliar faces. I prayed to God to watch over him and for someone to make him smile once in a while.

I grabbed my book and began to read. I just had to find out what decision Odysseus made between Scylla, the six-headed monster, and Charybdis, the whirlpool. If he chose Scylla he would lose six of his best men, and if he chose Charybdis they would all survive or all die. It all depended if Charybdis was swallowing the sea or not. It was a very difficult decision, but Odysseus made it choosing Scylla. I imagined myself as Odysseus, and I think that I would of risked it all—gone with Charybdis. It would of been a much bigger risk, but with the whirlpool there's a chance everyone survives. I couldn't of chosen Scylla and knew that fact that giving up six of my best men.

The door squeaked open and Lily peeked through the doorway. I gave a little squeal because I was at the part where one of the men was in Scylla's mouth. Lily jumped as I squealed.

"Oh sorry, Lily. I didn't mean to scare you," I giggled.

"No, no, I's shoulds of knockeds. But you's ready fo' bed."

I nodded as she came to me and pulled the covers right up to my neck, just the way I liked it.

"Goods night, Izzy," Lily said shutting the door.

"Good night Lily." But the door was already shut

Chapter 17

I woke up on a brand new day but not by the shake of Lily's hand. I woke up from a dream. I don't remember if it was a good one or not, but I sure was a sweating. I walked over to my bowl that was full of ice cold water and washed my face. I had to get all the sweat off. I wish I could of remembered what I dreamt. Lily walked in the room carrying shoes in her left hand.

"You's up alreadys Izzy." Lily was a little amazed that I got up without her waking me up. I rarely woke up on my own.

"I woke up from a dream I guess." I wiped my face with a towel.

"Whats a surprise. Oh, and Izzy, yous done left ya' shoes on da po'ch da other day. You's lucky I's got tem befo'e yous Mama did," Lily said.

"Oh gosh, thanks Lily. I mean it," I said knowing Mama would of darn bitten my head off if she saw those shoes.

Lily grinned one of her famous grins which just made you smile yourself.

I was at the breakfast table, and the conversations weren't that bad— not that I was in any of them. It was official that Governor Wilson Lumpkin was coming to the Wadsworth Estates a week from tomorrow which was Saturday. I was so excited that the governor would be having dinner with us. I remember some years before we had a governor eat with us, but I was too young to know anything or remember. I had a lot of questions I wanted to ask Governor Lumpkin.

After everyone left the dining room, I walked into the kitchen. Ann handed me a basket and said, "Fills da basket up with flowers. I's have a vase waitin' fo'e ya in da livin' room. You's put the flowers in da vase. Oh and Izzy, you's wear dat bonnet ya hear."

I strolled merrily along the dirt path wearing my white laces bonnet. I could see Emma, Ticey, and May putting all the cotton they plucked into one big sack.

"Izzy! Hey Izzy! Comes over here guh!" Emma shouted.

I trotted over to her to see what she wanted.

"Izzy, you's tell them some of thats stor'ie you's were tellin' me da other day. Tell dem about da adventu'es and da monsters," Emma said as all of their eyes got really big.

I got all excited to tell them. "Well, I'll tell y'all the story about Scylla, the six-headed monster, and Charybdis, the whirlpool. I told them about that adventure acting out all the parts. I also told them about how the adventurers almost had reached their home, Ithaca, but someone opened a bag of wind and it brought them even further back from home than before. I kept telling them stories until I ran out. I told them that I would read some more and then report what I read. They were soon getting up to go back to the fields because Emma said that she'd finished up with bagging cotton. I sat there with Emma and talked to her for a while. I told her how the governor was coming over and all. She wasn't too interested in that, but I told her I was.

"Izzy, did ya knows we's a gettin' two mo' slaves?" Emma asked me.

"I wouldn't of known anything except I heard Paps say at dinner the other day that he only got two. I figured he was talking about slaves."

"We's gettin' 'em later dis week." Emma said.

"Do you know if it's a man or woman." I asked her.

"Shore don't, buts we'll find out soon enough." Emma said.

I saw Phillip making his way over toward us, so I told Emma she better go because he said he'd whip her if he ever saw us two together again. He probably forgot that he ever said that because he ain't the brightest person, but it was safest if Emma left.

Phillip approached the table where I was still seated. "What was the nigger doin' over here with you?" Phillip asked as he took a big spit.

I didn't let Phillip intimidate me, so I knew how to handle situations with him. "Nothing worth questioning. Anything else that isn't your business you want to rub your nose in?" I suddenly wanted to hit myself because if he told Mama or Paps how rude I was, no telling how much trouble I would be in. Phillip didn't answer me he just kept staring.

"Well, if that's all I guess I'll be on my way," I said.

He didn't say anything back, and since it didn't look like he was moving any I got up and walked along the cornfield until Phillip walked away. He was heading toward the cane field just about the time I spotted Jones. Jones was carrying two big bags full of corn. He plopped them down on the table, and asked me to sit down with him. I was planning on doing it anyway so I sat on the seat across from him. He had two big tin bowls he was putting the corn in after he pealed it.

"Jones, let me take one of the bowls to the kitchen just in case Phillip sees me sitting here with you because he's been questioning me a lot lately," I said.

"Sounds good ta me," Jones said.

Changing the subject I asked, "You know what me and Emma found out?"

"No, buts I got a feelin' you's gonna tell me," Jones said grinning.

"No I ain't. I was just wandering if you knew or not," I said laughing.

"Now c'mon Izzy, I's anxious ta know what's ya talking about." Jones was trying to get me to tell him, and he succeeded.

"Well, I suppose I'll tell you. Emma and I found out that we getting two more slaves later this week."

"Emma is always da first ta find out 'bout stuff like dat," Jones said.

"I know." And I peeled another ear of corn.

Me and Jones just kept on talking about life and stuff. How one day I won't have to worry about talking to Jones and getting into trouble or having to lie my way out of it. We always wished for that day to hurry up and come. We kept talking away until I saw that Phillip was heading out of the cane field again. I told Jones that I'd best be on my way. I grabbed the bowl and my basket and was heading toward the porch when I realized that I had forgotten to pick flowers; I headed for the side of the house.

Chapter 18

Now, the side of the house was where the prettiest wild flowers in all the world are kept. That's what I liked to believe because I could not imagine lovelier flowers than those. I spotted the bunch that I was going pick; they were calling my name with the scent of their petals. Oh, the smell was so overwhelming. Suddenly, I heard foot-steps behind me, and at first I thought it was Phillip come to question me some more. Then I realized that it was Pete's shadow approaching; I remembered other times he snuck behind me and scared the living daylights out of me. Before he could come up behind me, I turned around so fast and yelled "CAUGHT YA!"

"Well, now Miss Izzy, I was so fer shorely quiet. How'd ya hear me?" Pete asked curiously.

"Pete why you weren't quiet a bit. I could hear you coming a mile away," I said jokingly.

"Awe shoot, Miss Izzy, I get ya next time." And Pete did a fancy bow that you see men doing to ladies. Pete was just doing it as a joke though.

"Pete, you wanna help me pick some of the prettiest flowers in the world."

"Can I?" Pete said being smart.

"Well, never mind Mr. Rude," I said even though I knew he was teasing.

Pete lifted one eyebrow up and then he winked. Soon we were both kneeling, and we were being so careful about the flowers we picked for not all made the rare selection. I don't recall if I mentioned this or not but the best thing about Pete was he took everything bad and put a smile behind it. He tried to make everything have happiness within it. That is such a special quality that he had. It made me look up to him in a way. Pete and I ended up sitting down on the old broken wagon after we picked the million-dollar flowers. He was such a inspirational person to talk to. Even though he wasn't well educated he knew what he wanted and what he was talking about. Why he could look at a death and bring light to that tragedy. After a while I told him that I should be heading back, and he looked at me and lifted one eyebrow.

"Miss Izzy, you ain't goin' no where 'till we race," Pete said trying to be all serious.

"You think you gonna win! Not this time." Me and Pete always raced but the reason I kept racing him was because he wasn't like all the other adults. Pete wouldn't let me win on purpose—I had to actually win. Well, I never won yet, but I was gonna get there one day.

He grabbed the bowl of corn, and I had the basket of flowers. I counted to three and off we went. First one to the front porch. It was only about three hundred yards. We were running so fast I couldn't even feel my legs below me. We were running and running and then we stopped.

Out of breath, "I almost had you… almost," I said.

"I know, I better practice harder." Pete said kinda laughing.

"Thanks, Pete."

"For what?"

"For not letting me win." Even though after every time we raced I always said "thanks Pete," it never failed that he asked "for what." Pete not letting me win was the only reason I kept racing him— for one day to have that glory of winning without any help; for the fact that I won on my own. The glory is worth so much, yet victory is priceless.

He handed me the basket of corn that he had been holding. Pete bowed and I curtsied, as if we were royalty. I walked slow up the big white porch steps dreading to go in. Three bodies inside with no surprise it, *Twas the Three Ladies*. They were sipping their tea as suspected. I glanced around the room looking for the vase, and before they could say anything, I scurried along and placed the glorious bouquet down gently in the vase as if the they were little babies fast asleep.

"That'll brighten the room up. I thought the room needed a little color. Didn't you? Well, that makes everything much better." I said being overly cheery.

"Ah, yes—- Oh yes——Hmm.." The comments that came out of the three ladies' mouths. I didn't know who said what or even if those were the exact comments, but I know that they were very casual. When they spoke there was a bit of astonishment. And before they could ask about the bowl of corn I said, "Oh and the corn I got especially for the governor. I mean the governor can't simply come to the Wadsworth plantation and not have some of the finest corn he ever will put in his mouth." Now I never tasted corn from anywhere else, but I just had a feeling that this here corn was the best.

The response from the three ladies was the same as the first, casual with a bit of astonishment. I looked for a moment at them, took my time staring at them, then I turned around and left the room. I walked into the kitchen to sit and talk with Lily and Ann before Mama or Grandma had me play the piano for another hundred hours. It really brought the love out of playing an instrument.

Chapter 19

Sunday morning was a new day and promised a new beginning. One shake of the soft sugary hand of Lily and I was up.

"Morning Lily," I said yawning. I was stretching so hard; I lifted my two arms above my head as they touched Canada.

Sunday mornings were always soothing for me. I would go to church and ask the Lord for mercy on my soul. Mama always told me I needed more mercy than anyone, that didn't always make me feel too good. After breakfast we got into the buggy, which Pete drove, and went to church. Paps didn't allow us to bring any other slaves with us besides Pete. Pete drove us there, but he wasn't allowed in. No slaves were allowed in. To me it never made much sense because in the Bible it says God invites all to Him and His kingdom. For some reason the slaves were always excluded from the "all." The pastor was a nice man with two boys of his own. His children were real nice looking on the outside. They would even pretend to be nice in front of elder folks, but the truth is that they were cruel when no one was looking. Not one adult could ever believe that though because they were such "nice looking" young men.

When I am inside God's house I always tried to listen real hard for His voice. I don't know why, but I pictured trumpets in the background and a loud call from the heavens, but that ain't it at all. I soon learned God can answer us through other people, and sometimes when you're asking stuff He answers in tiny whispers. So soon I stopped doing all the talking when I prayed, and I allowed God to talk for once. And He did, just like Miss Laura told me He would. It was a soft tiny whisper.

After the pastor's sermon, it was time to go home. I felt awfully bad when we got back outside, and I saw Pete sweating up a storm. He was just sitting there, just the way we left him in the blazing hot sun. The way back home didn't seem as long. That always seems so, don't you think? I never knew why either.

Some people say it's because you're so excited about getting there it takes longer, but I don't find that true because one time we were invited to go to the Wilson's, and I would have rather been sick that night because those weren't the nicest people in the world. It seemed to take forever to get there…well there I go rambling again. Sorry I do tend to drift off. If you haven't gotten use to it yet, please forgive me.

When we were back home, I told myself that I had better finish that essay because I knew that Miss Laura was coming Monday morning. I opened the Bible to the first verse I saw, and it was Psalms 51:10 *Create in me a clean heart, O God, And renew a steadfast spirit within me.* I said those words to myself two or three times before I wrote it down on paper. I interpreted it as Lord give me a clean heart, that will not see hatred. God keep my heart pure from evil, and a clean spirit that will last forever.

That night in my bed I thought about the day and how I lived it—if I lived it well or not or if I even lived it at all. Miss Laura told me once you should never let days go by unworked, without dreams, without some sort of compassion in what you do, and without challenges. I admit that plenty of my days slipped away without work, dreams, compassion, and challenges, but every new day I will try, try again.

That Monday morning after breakfast, I was walking towards the library to wait for Miss Laura when she rounded the corner.

"Hey, Miss Laura!" I said in a merry expression.

"Hey, yourself," Miss Laura said right back at me.

We walked into the library together both taking our seats.

"Are you ready to finish the <u>Odyssey</u>?" Miss Laura asked me.

Nodding my head vigorously saying, "Of course."

"Good, but first let me see the essay you did on a Bible verse."

"Alright," I said handing her paper. I always kinda got a little nervous about handing a paper in because I would usually love the work I did. I was always scared that Miss Laura wouldn't appreciate it as I did. Some of my best work was overlooked. As she finished reading it, her eyes came off the paper and on to me.

"Izzy I really like the verse you chose." She seemed to be pleased, but she still didn't say anything about the way I explained the verse.

Miss Laura reached down into her bag and got out the <u>Odyssey</u>, and I got mine. I was ready to get to the end; I was excited to see what would happen. I felt my eyes getting bigger and bigger as we got deeper into the pages. Soon Odysseus had to fight off a hundred suitors that were after his wife. After he did that, his wife had to make sure that it was really him because she hadn't seen her husband in twenty long years. When she finally realized that it was really him, they held each other forever. When Miss Laura read those last words in the book, I was thrilled. I wasn't thrilled because the book was over, but thrilled because it was great.

"Izzy, you know you really finished this book pretty fast. Did you understand it all?"

"I think so."

"It's very important that you did. Remember what I told you about not how you shouldn't just read a book, but read between the lines."

"Yes, I remember."

"Good. I want you to write a paper comparing some of the adventures and characters with your own life. I want this paper to come straight from your heart. It really needs to be special. Now, today is Monday and I will give you until Saturday. That should be enough time. I'm not going to give you a certain length because you might be able to say all you need in a couple paragraphs or could be ten pages." She looked at me and her eyes grew larger.

"I understand Miss Laura," I said.

"Good, now my sweet, I will see you on Wednesday. Now until then, keep your smile." And she held my face in her palm.

"Bye Miss Laura," I said as she went out the door. I looked through the window and watched her leave on the buggy.

Chapter 20

I sat there thinking of how I was going to compare my simple life with the life of Odysseus. How would I compare his complicated life full of adventures with my life? I sat there thinking how I would do it and jotting down ideas onto paper.

After dinner I ran outside to breathe in the mellow evening air that I so loved. I kicked my shoes off, and I walked slowly along the dirt path letting the dirt creep in between my toes. A strong wind pushed me back a little, and I closed my eyes and thanked God for this wonderful life He gave me and for never giving up on me no matter how many times I would fail doing good.

"Hey, there," I called when I was about fifteen feet away from Ole Uncle.

"Why Miss Izzy, how ya doin'?" He said in his deep southern voice.

"I'm doing," I said swinging one leg back and forth.

"Would ya likes me ta fix ya some water?" He asked pointing to the well.

"No thanks, I'm not too thirsty right now."

"Oh alright, I's just offering."

Me and Ole Uncle just sat there talking to each other 'bout certain things, and I guess we drifted off to the subject on families. He said that some people belonged to your family even though they weren't of your own blood. I liked that. I liked the thought that somewhere a family loved me—somewhere I belonged.

After a while, Ole Uncle needed to get back to work so I decided to walk to the peach tree which was closest to the cane field. If you ever see peach tree my best advice is to first to take a peach and then draw a picture of the tree. A peach tree is just so lovely. I can't imagine how exquisite a whole orchard of peach trees would look. I jumped up pretty high to reach it. I bit right into the peach and broke the rough skin and let the sweetness dissolve inside of my mouth. Paps told me once when I was little, and when I was an interest in his life, that there was no other peach quite like a Georgia peach. I believed him because I couldn't see how any other peach could be so satisfying. I spotted Emma walking towards the benches. I ran up to her because she was carrying a number of bags, and it looked like she was going to drop one.

"Need some help?" I asked her.

"Shore," She said handing me a bag full of cotton. "This ones good," pointing to the table on the far left. I always liked that about Emma she wasn't too prideful to admit that she needed help when she did, and just because I was white, it didn't stop her from accepting the help. When someone is willing to offer help, she was always glad to go ahead and take it.

"Thanks Iz. Good gracious, it's hot," Emma said taking a seat on the bench.

"Yeah, but not as hot as yesterday."

"Yous right." Emma said as I giggled. She let out a big yawn; she must of been real tired. She looked pretty worn out. I didn't stay much longer because she had to get more loads of cotton, and I didn't want to keep her from it and then get her into trouble.

I slowly walked back to the house letting my feet drag behind me. I started drifting off thinking about how Odysseus and his men had to sail the deep blue sea and all the times they got lost on their way. Odysseus was suddenly erased from my mind when I saw the white sheets that were whiter than the clouds. They were hanging up on a clothes line. The scent was a strong, lemony smell. I danced with the sheets as I ran beneath them. I danced to the music that was coming from the heavens. It was almost as if it was relieving to run between and dance with the freshly dried sheets. I hoped that I never got too old to dance, too old to dream.

I walked through the kitchen door and there were Lily and Ann cooking a nice big supper as usual. Without even asking, Lily fixed me a cold glass of iced lemonade. There was nothing

like a glass full of cold lemonade on hot summer days. The pulp
tickled my throat as it went down. Lily and Ann were laughing
as they saw me start my third glass.

"Ya shore is thirsty, huh!" Ann said to me.

I nodded taking another sip, "I sure am."

"Izzy, ya goes and make yer self looks real nice fer supper,
Lily said.

As I walked into the living room, I remembered I left my
shoes on the front porch again. After I got my shoes, I thought I
would write some more on that paper Miss Laura assigned to
me. This time when I began to write everything became so clear.
How I placed Odysseus's adventures into my life. I began to see
what Miss Laura was talking about. Soon I couldn't seem to put
my pen down. Thoughts kept entering my mind and I tried to put
it all down on paper.

I soon was getting ready for supper. I was combing my hair
until it felt like silk. I thought that since I was already in front of
the mirror I might as well give it another shot; I was gonna try
reading myself again. I took a deep breath and put all the
strength that I had and stared deep within myself. I met failure
once again. I grew so frustrated because I didn't understand how
I couldn't read myself when I thought I could read everyone
else. Why I asked, why couldn't I be more like Odysseus? He
knew what was inside of him; he knew what he was made of.
Odysseus knew all of his strengths and weaknesses. Why was it
I was only finding my weak points?

Chapter 21

Wednesday morning I woke up with a breeze of a new beginning. I had one of those dreams where your whole body just feels refreshed. It made my heart beat faster than ever. It felt good; I felt real good! I danced over to the window, opening it to let all the fresh air fill my room. What a magnificant peace it gave me. I turned around because I heard my door open.

"Izzy, you's ups already." Lily was so shocked because it was seldom that I woke up on my own.

"Yes!" I responded with so much joy. "Isn't this the most beautiful day you ever saw." I threw my arms up in the air and leaned my head back.

She nodded a little confused. "Izzy ya feelin' alrights?" She asked a bit worried.

"Do I feel alright? I feel great! I feel alive. Why don't I feel like this every single day? Oh Lily!"

She shook her head, "you's best get dressed right now, Izzy."

"Lily, how could I possibly get dressed right now. I just couldn't." I started doing turns and singing and twirling. Lily tried to stop me, but instead I grabbed her and we started dancing together. I felt so revived; I felt the gift of life. I was filled with much joy.

"Izzy, what's gotten inta ya? I's gonna gets us both inta trouble. If ya Mama sees me like this dancin' and alls." Lily was a little nervous.

"Lily, who cares! Just keep dancing," I said as we both started laughing. Lily was soon getting more into it. I felt like I was on top of the world, like I could do anything I wanted. But then our four eyes turned to the doorway and saw Mama. I heard both of our hearts drop.

"I hope I didn't interrupt anything," Mama said in a voice that was so sarcastic that just made you feel stupid.

"No, no, no, mam," Lily said hesitating a bit.

"Well, why wasn't I invited to this little party," Mama said in such a cold voice that I could hear the ice break.

"Mama, I'm sorry it's my fault. I woke up this morning feeling so good that I was twirling and singing. Why, I just pulled Lily right into it because I wanted to share my happiness with someone."

"Lily, you are lucky I am not putting the whip to you, but hear this if I ever see you doing anything like this ever again there is no doubt in my mind that you will be whipped even if I have to— I'll whip you myself. You're making me sick just looking at you; leave immediately." Mama said very stern manner.

"Yes Mistress." And Lily left the room swiftly.

Before I could say anything, Mama jumped at me. "Isabel Wadsworth there is no excuse that is good enough for what you did. You disgust me. Just think if your Papa saw you singing and dancing with a nigger, and even taking up for one! I can't believe you! Do you ever think?" She kept barking at me. She was sure good at making people feel really small and worthless. Even if someone was ten times bigger than she was she could still make them feel as small as a pea.

"Mama I was just so ha—" She cut me off before I could say anything else.

"I don't want to hear another word out of you. In fact I don't want to see your face at breakfast this morning. You can eat with the niggers for all I care since you like them so much." Right after she said that she left the room and slammed the door behind her. I didn't budge until I couldn't hear my Mama's footsteps anymore. After that, some of that good feeling that I woke up with was gone, but I didn't allow it all to run away from me. I wasn't about to cry or even let her upset me too much because I got pretty used to my Mama yelling at me like that.

After I slowly got dressed, I headed downstairs. Everyone was going into the dining room for breakfast but me. I decided I would play the piano until everyone was finished with breakfast.

I loved playing the piano when I wasn't forced. I closed my eyes and let the music flow through my fingers.

After they were all finished with breakfast, Mama, Grandma, and Sarah were getting ready to go into town to get themselves dresses and also a new linen table cover for the dining room. I walked into the dining room where I saw Lily and Ann cleaning off the table. Lily placed a plate of food for me on the table so I could have my breakfast. I told Lily from the bottom of my heart that I was sorry, and she, sweet as she is, said there was no reason for me to be sorry. When I was finished with my breakfast, I thanked them for saving me a plate. They told me it was no problem. By that time I forgot that it was Wednesday and it was about the time Miss Laura usually came. I quickly ran to the library, and there sat Miss Laura. She said that she hadn't been there that long. I was happy she didn't ask why I was late because I really didn't feel like explaining. She taught me about the history in the early 1600's which was quite fascinating. Although, most everything Miss Laura taught was fascinating.

"Isabel, hon, how is your paper coming around?"

"I think it's turning out pretty good, in fact I think it's turning out real good."

"Lovely, dear."

It wasn't too much longer before Miss Laura was on her way. I didn't feel like I would do a good job if I wrote the paper now, so I didn't. When I didn't feel hundred percent into something I tried not to do it because all my effort wouldn't of been in it. Instead, I decided to go outside. I opened the door onto the front porch and just decided to sit on the gigantic white wooden rocking chair which had a great view to the fields. I have to admit the plantation was gorgeous looking from afar, but when you got up close and saw and heard everyone's sad stories the beauty kinda evaporated.

I saw that Paps and Joseph were looking at something from a distance, but I couldn't tell what it was. Then I saw the wagon that was coming up the dirt road towards Paps and Joseph. Joseph was jumping up and down because he was so excited.

Suddenly I remembered about the two slaves that were coming in. As the wagon was getting closer to Paps and Joseph, the more excited Joseph would get. I could of sworn it was his birthday or something.

"Papa, the niggers are here! Those are them right there, aren't they?" Joseph asked Paps like if those weren't the slaves, he was just going to die.

"Yes, son, these are the niggers," Paps said in such a proud voice.

Matthew was in the wagon which was being driven by Pete. Matthew hopped in the back to get the two slaves out.

"Get up, boy!" Paps yelled into the center of the wagon. He grew frustrated and shoved the wedge of his rifle into the center of the wagon hitting one of the slaves. Shortly after that the two men stood up a little shakily because both of their hands and feet were tied together. There was one that looked like he was in his twenties and the other could of been in his early forties.

"C'mon boy!" Paps would yell and shove one of them with his rifle. Paps expected this to bother them but it didn't. They were probably used to it, but that made Paps madder than ever. He thought that he would teach them a lesson. He yelled for Matthew to get the whip. Paps was going to whip them because he needed to feel more powerful and in control. Joseph was whooping away because he knew that the slaves were about to be beaten. Joseph was only around the age of six then, and I felt that he shouldn't be open to this sort of violence and hatred. The worst thing of all was Joseph's reaction to all of it, instead of the average six year old being frightened, Joseph was thrilled. Both of the slaves dragged along to the spot where they would be whipped. It was so heartbreaking. Their faces showed no expression. I followed them to where Paps would begin the whipping.

"These the niggers?" Phillip asked as he spit purposely onto the younger one's foot.

"Yeah," Matthew said as he grabbed the older one first and put his tied hands onto a hook on a pole. The hook on the pole was high so it made the person stand on the tiptop of their toes. He did the same to the younger one also. When Matthew ripped off their shirts, I gasped as I saw the scars on their backs. Both of the men had so many, too many. Phillip pulled back on the whip and slung it across and whipped them one and then the other. It was all too horrifying. To this day, I do not see how a six-year old child wouldn't be frightened or even in tears, but Joseph was cheering it on. I had to push down the pain in my throat because it was sad to see it actually happen to someone. If you never saw it happen to someone right before your eyes then you really can't have a big opinion on it. Well, that's my personal thought. Just to think if it was that bad to watch no telling how horrible it was to be in the shoes of those who were beat.

When Paps thought they had suffered enough, he told Phillip to stop. Paps, Phillip, and Matthew were soon away from the sight. Charles untied the men but felt no remorse for them. Emma went up to the men with wet rags when Charles left. She was going to tend to the sores.

I saw Joseph trailing along behind Paps towards the house. I thought that I would catch up and stop Joseph. "Joseph! Joseph wait up!" I yelled to him.

He stopped and turned around, "What you want Isabel?" He said in a high little voice.

When I finally caught up, I asked him, "Did you think that was funny?"

"You mean watching those niggers get beat? Yeah, dat was great! It was so much fun," He said getting a little too excited.

"You found that enjoyable?!" I said losing my patience. "Watching a person get-ting beaten for no reason is fun to you? So in other words you like to see people suffer. Entertainment for you is the suffering and agony of others. When someone cries for help you'll just whoop for more? Two men who did nothing wrong just got beaten, beaten bad, and you want to see more? Joseph, you wanted an encore to see people being destroyed and torn apart inside and out. Joseph that's monsterous; instead hollering for more, you should of seen what you could do for them." As I kept talking, my anger grew inside me. "Well, hear this Joseph Wadsworth, if you call those men niggers than you are not worthy to be called a nigger." I didn't mean to hurt his feelings, but I had all this rage. I grew even angrier and sadder when I was thinking of what my baby brother was growing up to be.

Trying not to care, he stuck his tongue out at me which was typical for Joseph. Then he started to cry, and I found that normal for him only being six. He ran all the way back to the house. I had no doubt in my mind that he went straight to tell Paps.

"What did I do? What did I do?" I whispered softly to myself for I knew I would be in serious trouble when Joseph would tell Paps.

Chapter 22

My mind escaped me and so did my appetite because I totally forgot about supper. I let myself drift and drift without thoughts. When I reached the cornfield, I shook my head several times because I felt as if I was in some sort of trance. Thoughts revisited my mind, and I thought of how the day started off as pure as gold and slowly was turning into rust.

I saw Jones working in the cornfield, and I longed to run to him and cry to him. I wanted to tell him everything that's been bothering me, but as usual, I pushed it back, smiled and told him everything was fine and dandy. We immediately started talking. Oh, we talked about flying, the sunrises and sunsets, and the new slaves, Joe being older one and Sam the younger fellow. Then, we started talking about dreams and wishes; not much later we started talking about the Bible. I think Jones sensed that something was bothering me, but he knew that if I didn't mention it that I probably didn't want to talk about it. I knew that it was good to talk about stuff and to let it all out, but I also knew that it wasn't good to force things out. For one thing the holder of the problem needs to be willing to talk about it because if they're not nothing will change. So we didn't bring any of our problems up. Another reason I didn't like talking about my problems with Jones was because I felt so selfish. I mean there I was having all I could ever need, and there Jones was a slave who was treated like an animal. I knew Jones would understand if I told him, but it just didn't feel right telling my sad stories to someone who was treated much worse than I was.

We were watching the sun set as I yelped, "Oh my goodness! Oh my goodness!"

"What is it Izzy?" Jones asked.

"I can't stay a minute longer I have to run. I haven't been in all day. I missed supper!"

"You best hurry, Izzy!"

I ran and ran until I reached the front door of hell. Fear was within me as I crept inside the living room. There stood the trial, the two judges, Mama and Paps. The prosecutor being Joseph and the jury was my Grandma. Sarah was not quite part of the trial, but she stood in the far left of the room just watching. Since this didn't mean anything to Sarah, she didn't take much interest being she really only thought of herself. I looked at my parents, the two volcanos ready to burst. My heart was beating faster and faster each second as I waited for one to speak. I would have usually spoken first, but in this situation if I did, it would of been off with my head. I tried to walk closer to them, but my feet wouldn't budge; it felt as if they were cemented to the ground.

My Paps was the first to speak, which was unusual I suspected my Mama. "Just who the hell do you think are? Huh? Just who the hell do you think you are, young lady? Telling your little brother that he isn't worthy to be called a nigger." He had to stop for a minute because he was filled with so much indignation that I thought he was going to blow.

I tried to speak, but I couldn't; there was nothing. I opened my mouth, but no words would come out. I felt there was nothing I could say to make the situation better. Was I sorry for what I said? I spoke my mind, which did usually get me into trouble. I was sorry that I spoke harshly to Joseph when I did. I should of used a better tone, but sorry for the words I chose? Sadly, I was not.

Paps soon got back to what he was saying, "And this morning your Mother told me that you were singing and dancing with a nigger. Do you want other people to think that this house had nigger lovers! You make your Mother and I just sick, just plan sick!" By this time Paps was so close to me that I was getting showered when he spoke. I was just shaken up quite a bit that Paps words were becoming a blur. I did see it coming though. Paps held his hand back and struck me across the face. My stomach churned. Paps never hit me before. I was more shocked than hurt, but don't get me wrong— it hurt. I swallowed down all the pain that was there. I didn't want to show them that they hurt me.

"Get out of my sight." Paps last words from the trial.

I walked up very slowly because I felt sick to my stomach. I knew Mama was happy that Paps said what he said. She didn't even have to say anything; she was so pleased with what Paps said to me. Man, how the day began with all smiles and was ending in a thunderstorm. I climbed in my bed and fell asleep right there. I knew I wouldn't be getting supper anyhow. Later that night, Lily sneaked in and woke me up and gave me a buttered roll. She was always thinking of me; she was such a sweetheart. I tried to let those words that Paps spoke to me escape me, but somehow they wouldn't. I shouldn't of let them bother me, but those words pinched my heart.

Chapter 23

The next morning I woke up in the clothes I wore last night. Lily came into the room and got me up. She walked me to the bowl, and pulled my hair back very gently as she dunked my head under the cold water. She patted my back and began singing. When she was all done, she looked at me smiled and held me tight in her arms.

"Izzy, ya Mama says dat you's to stay up here today. I's bring all yer food, but ya ain't allowed ta leave," she paused. "Butcha know if ya needs anythings I's get it fer ya." Lily said as she rubbed my back, "I's be back soon with yer breakfast."

A lump was caught in my throat, and this time it wouldn't work by me just pushing it down. I quickly drank the water that was in the bowl to push down the lump that was stuck. I thought how would Pete look at this situation and make good of it. I thought for a minute or two and realized that I could finish my paper that I had started, and I could put all my time into it. I put all my efforts into this paper because I wanted this to be spectacular. It took me quite a while to finish because I can't translate that well the thoughts in my head onto paper. When the thoughts sit inside my head, they seemed perfect. Then, when I put them on paper it is as if nothing made sense.

Lily was comforting. She came and brought me, breakfast, dinner, supper, and and snacks that day. The day really didn't seem long because I spent the whole time finishing my paper which I was very proud of. I never bragged, and never did I tell anyone that I was proud. I kept the secrets to myself. When I was in bed that night, I realized that that was the first day I spent the entire day in my room. Because even when I was ill, I would always go outside and let Mother Nature heal my sickness.

The next morning when Lily woke me up, I thought that the first thing I would do would be run down the stairs and out the door. That was not the case because I was prohibited to leave my room once again.

"Did she say," I paused. "Did she say if I could go down for supper."

"Izzy, sorry hon, but she said ya can't leave da room da whole day," Lily said feeling sorry for me, and that is not what I wanted. I didn't want anyone to feel sorry for me.

"Is the governor still coming tonight?" I asked.

"Yeah, he is."

"And I can't leave the room."

"Ya Mama won't allow it. Oh Izzy, I knows ya were lookin' fo'ward ta seein' the governor. I tell ya what, I's tell ya everythang dat hap'ens. I's tell ya e'ery move he makes and e'ery word he says."

"Thanks, Lily," I said more cheerful.

"Ah, I knows dat yous would do dat fo' me."

"Wait, what about Miss Laura isn't she coming today? Can I still go to the library?"

"Oh yeah, ya can, but yer Mama says if she sees ya, it's gonna bes another two days in da bedroom. I say right afta Miss Laura is done go straight upstairs."

"Alright."

"Oh Izzy, I knows ya better than dat. You's thinkin' that ya can go outside just fo' a minute and not gets caught. Izzy dontcha do dat."

"I won't," I said kinda smiling cause that was exactly what I was thinking.

"Promise me Izzy."

"I promise."

Chapter 24

I was happy that today was Saturday because I really wanted to talk to Miss Laura. She was the only white person that I knew that saw things the way I did. She thought that we were all equal too and how no person is better than the next. I guess that's because she is really into God. You might think— oh well, the pastor is into God, too, then he must see things that way also, but that is not always the case. There is a difference between knowing the facts in the Bible and knowing what's meant in between the lines, actually knowing God. Miss Laura knew about Emma being my best friend and Jones my soul mate. (Oh, I don't think I mentioned this. Don't be getting the wrong idea when I say soul mate. I know that term is used quite frequently when speaking of two people that are lovers. The definition is an intimate associate or companion, and that is what we were— companions.) Me and Emma were best friends, but me and Jones just had a special bond. If Mama or Paps ever found out who my friends were, why they would of killed me. Mama and Paps never ever understood. Mama always told me who I should be friends with and that just drove me crazy because I was the only person that knew what I truly looked for in others.

Soon it was time for me to hand in my paper. I was nervous because I wanted her to really like it. I thought about the Cyclops in my paper—the Cyclops in my life was my Mama. I didn't hate my Mama; I loved her, but she was a giant in my life as the Cyclops is a giant. In the story Odysseus blinds the Cyclops, but in my life I haven't yet blinded her. Now I don't literally want to blind her, but I want to some how reach out to her and make her realize it is the inside that counts in a person. Mama chooses the outside of people and if she was blind she wouldn't know who to hate. The Scylla and Charybdis, the hard decision, in my life was following the ways of my family or the path that I knew was right and would lead me to God. The longing that Odysseus had to go back to his home after twenty years, I compared with my longing for people to use their hearts and not be judgmental with the color of someone's skin. Poseidon, the king of the sea, who made Odysseus's journey home even harder I compared with my Paps and Grandma who didn't understand my views so immediately they "knew" it was wrong and gave me a tougher time. It went on and on, but those or just a few that I remember. Although, I do remember Miss Laura loving every word I chose. She even asked me if she could keep it. I was honored that she even wanted to keep one of my works; she never did before.

That evening when Governor William Lumpkin came over for supper, I was in my bedroom with a supper of my own. I wanted to be in the dining room listening to a lecture from the governor. Now you might be thinking, why in the world would you want to listen to a lecture? Well, lectures are quite fascinating; they are only boring if you allow them to be. I'm not talking about the lecturing you get when you're in trouble because we all hate those. I'm referring to the lectures you get from a person who is teaching, telling, or even giving an opinion on a certain subject. You see, Governor Lumpkin was a very intelligent and interesting man. He was one of the best speakers in Georgia at that time. There could be a room filled with a hundred people and you could hear a pen drop because everyone was so in tune with him. I was at the stairway trying to listen to what they were saying, but I couldn't make out any of the words.

Chapter 25

Monday morning I was allowed to eat with my family again, but I was not permited to speak. I wasn't allowed to go outside; I was only allowed to play the piano and go to the library when Miss Laura came. Otherwise, I sat at the window, running through the fields in my mind. I could feel the sun beam upon my fair skin.

The weeks seemed to slip by, and summer was running away from me. Fall was creeping into my life. I would pass by a window, and my eyes would dream about the outside world. How beautiful it was; it was as if I never noticed that before. I sometimes would sit and watch the leaves fall off the trees onto the ground. The green leaves were slowly fading to autumn colors.

It felt like a year before I was allowed back outside. The reason I was soon permitted to go back outside was because Mama was getting tired of me around the house so much. At the time I really didn't care for the reason; I was just happy that I could go back to my dreamland. When I heard the good news, I went straight for the door yelling thank you. I swung the door open and stepped my feet onto the porch. I tell you, that felt as if I was reborn; it felt truly glorious. The wind was now much thicker than usual. I didn't waste my time. The first thing I did was run over to the cornfields to see Jones. It felt as if I hadn't seen him in a century.

"Jones! Hey Jones!" I called out to him.

Jones turned around and looked real surprised. "Izzy! Well Izzy, I was beginning ta thinks dat I was never gonna sees you! How ya doin' guh?" He said smiling bigger than ever.

I ran over to him and hugged him tight. He held me in his arms, and we started doing turns. We couldn't stop laughing.

"Jones, I missed you too much," I said getting all sentimental.

"Izzy, I's missed ya too much, too. I's missed ya a whole lot," Jones said rubbing my head.

I swear that me and Jones talked for weeks that afternoon. We tried to catch up with all the missed time. Before Jones had to get back to work we flew. We flew through the fields. Our hands were firmly grasped as we tried to outrun the sun. We closed our eyes and soared through the fields flying away from all of our troubles. As we came in for a landing back to earth, I gave him another hug, and I let him get back to his work. I trailed out of the cornfields with a feeling so good that I could of danced on the moon. I walked over to the bench where I saw Emma.

I called out to her, "Hey Emma!"

"Hey guh!" Emma said happy to see me.

We tried to make up for all the lost time we had. I explained everything that happened. She knew most of it because she was the one who told Jones I wasn't allowed to go outside. We talked for a while longer, and then I walked her back to the cotton field because she needed to get back to work. When me and Emma departed, I decided to go to old oak and sit on one of her visible roots. I was trying to make up for weeks and weeks in one day.

Walking back from old oak, I wasn't paying any attention and I bumped into Ole Uncle. We said our hellos and had a short conversation, and then we said our goodbyes. I thought that it was such a beautiful day that I couldn't waste a second of it. I figured I should go and get the last bunch of wild flowers before they were all gone. Walking over to the best spot to pick the flowers, I saw Pete and Sam. Me and Pete talked for a good while. I tried to talk to Sam by introducing myself, but he said he didn't want anything to do with me. I was stunned when he said that. I have to admit that hurt a bit and surprised me

Chapter 26

The next couple of weeks went by, and me and Jones would have our talks in our special spot. Phillip would sometimes see us and it was getting hard to make up excuses. He was getting quite suspicious. He stopped falling for some of my excuses. I told Jones that maybe we should stop having our talks and all. Jones said that I was his best friend, and if he could not see his best friend anymore than there was no point to do anything. He insisted that I kept coming. One day it was one too many times, and Phillip told Paps that he was seeing me and Jones together a little too much. Paps first thought was Jones was doing sexual things to me which was absurd. Paps couldn't see the fact that I had a friend that was older and black. Paps just thought I was covering up for him. I tried to explain that Jones would never ever do that, but I couldn't get it through to Paps nor Mama. I had this gut feeling that one day would be the last day I would see Jones. I thought Paps and Mama were gonna have him sold because of what Phillip told them. My parents would rather believe Phillip, who had probably half a brain and said that Jones touched me sexually than me who said Jones was just a friend.

I woke up Thursday morning getting dressed to go eat breakfast. I had to wait until the rest of my family was finished because they didn't want me in there with them. They didn't want to have to look at me that long. After I had my breakfast hardly touching any of it, I went outside to the cornfield to speak to Jones. You might be thinking why go and see Jones when he was getting blamed for this. Jones wanted me to see him because he knew he might never see me again plus I told you earlier it was impossible to separate us.

"Hey Izzy," Jones said in a friendly voice but that was Jones for you, though. He could be getting eaten by bears but he would still be smiling. Jones knew that I was upset about the whole thing with Phillip and the horrible things he was spreading.

"Izzy there's nothing ta worries about it's gonna all be's alright."

"Jones, that's just the thing; it's not going to be alright. My Paps has just been madder than ever, and I can tell he's going to do something just awful, Jones, just awful. Jones, why don't you just run away. You could runaway and be free like we always talked about. You could be free like when we run through the cornfields and fly; we're free then. Jones, you could be like that. You could fulfill your dream of being a free man." The more I talked about Jones running away the more I thought it was a great idea. I thought that it seemed so perfect.

"Izzy what's ya sayin'? Shore I's loves ta be free, but Izzy runnin' away and hidin', that ain't no dream of mine. Say I's ran away where would I go? What would I's eat? Where would I's sleep? Izzy I believe dat I's a man; well shore I ain't as rich as ya Paps. I ain't got things like ya Paps, but I's believes I's a man likes him. Shore we different on da outside, but I's believes we da same person, da same man. I believe dat we equal, and since I says I's a man I's better acts like a man. Izzy, if they wants ta punish me, well, I ain't gonna fights back, but I shore as hell ain't gonna runaway and hidin'. I's gonna stay here and be's a man. They say I's ain't no man, well, dis gonna prove ta them dat I's am a man. They mights not like ta admit it, but Izzy they wills know I's a man. Now I's knows yous shouldn't have ta prove youself ta nobody, but I's showin' dem dat I's gonna stick it out Izzy." Jones said that meaning every single word of it. He was always true to his words.

"Jones, but they might, they could hurt you real bad. Why Jones they might even," I couldn't bring myself to say it, "Jones they might try to kill you." My voice was shaky.

"Then they gonna haves ta kill a man," Jones said a little shaken up himself.

I wanted to breakdown right then and there in his arms, but I didn't. I did what I usually did and pushed it down and swallowed it up. "Oh Jones," I said softly as I pulled him down and squeezed him tight. I thought that it might be the last time I could really hug him.

"Izzy, they ain't gonna hurt me. I's won't let dem; I's too strong fer dem ta hurts me. So don't yous a go worryin' 'bout it," Jones said with his hands on my shoulder. I nodded my head. "But Izzy if dey do hurts me, and takes me froms dis earth, well, ya taught me about God. And ya said if I's believe and gots faith then I's will go ta heaven. Well, Izzy I's wait fer ya fer ever. I means I's wait till yous get ta heaven too," Jones said staring deep into my eyes.

I started thinking of what really might happen to Jones and I grew more afraid. I shook my head and we embraced.

Jones whispered in my ear, "Until heaven Izzy, until heaven." My heartbeat was getting faster and faster by the second, and I had to take deep breaths in order to keep breathing. Jones was my soul mate; I couldn't bare to think what I would do without him. I needed him just as much as he needed me. I looked up at him and saw a tear coming down his left eye.

"Jones, don't cry, please." I could barely finish what I was saying.

"It's alright Izzy, I's don't mind. One day yous won't either," Jones said as the tears fell down his cheek.

"Jones, you call yourself an equal man to my Paps, well you're not. You a better man than my Paps," I said slowly taking deep breaths.

Jones smiled and patted my back and motioned for me to go. I always understood why Jones needed me to leave. He needed to be alone for awhile. I ran off to be with myself too. I just sat thinking of what could happen. It hurt to think too long so I didn't.

That night I just couldn't get to sleep. I was sweating like crazy. My mind kept racing; I just couldn't keep calm. I was still awake when Lily came into tuck me in. When I finally fell asleep, I awakened an hour later sweating even harder from a bad dream. A dream I was scared would become reality.

Chapter 27

I woke up in a frantic the next morning. I knew if Paps was going to do anything at all he was going to do it early in the morning. I hopped out of bed so fast that I didn't even think about changing. I ran downstairs and flew out the house. I first looked to where Cranby and Ticey were when Junior got sold, but no one was there. I then ran straight to the place where Sam and Joe had been beaten. There was a crowd there. I saw that Jones was already tied up, and Paps had already begun to whip him. I felt responsible as Paps would pull the whip back and slash Jones. The arm of my Paps was whipping as hard and as fast as he could. My heart sank to the bottom of my knees; I felt weak as could be. Seeing your best friend, your soul mate getting beat for something he did not do was unbearable.

"Say it!" Phillip snarled.

Jones shook his head.

"Say that you sexually molested Isabel Wadsworth, Daniel Wadsworth's daughter!" Phillip yelled.

Jones shook his head again. This angered Paps so he began to whip faster and harder. The bleeding grew heavier.

"Stubborn son-of-a-bitch!" Paps yelled and Matthew, Phillip, and Charles all nodded.

I felt like I had to say something or do something. I felt responsible. "It's not true. He never touched me in that way. They are all lies!" It was the only thing that I could think of to say.

"Shut up, Isabel! Go inside!" Paps yelled to me.

"Please stop, it's not true!" I said begging for them to stop.

"God damn it, Isabel go inside now!" Paps screamed on the top of his lungs.

I began to run towards Jones to save him; I wanted to untie him. I needed to do something. As I was running toward Jones, Cranby grabbed my shoulders. He whispered in my ear, "There's nothing we can do now to stop this. I'm sorry, but there is nothing we can do now." I imagine that was the same thing he had to tell Ticey as she was running to save her baby, Junior.

Cranby and I sneaked to a different side so Paps couldn't see me. I could see Jones's face where I was now standing. I thought to myself he had aged so much, or maybe it was that I never noticed.

"He sure as hell ain't letting go. Might take forever to kill this bastard." Phillip said to Paps. Jones was so strong he sure wasn't letting go; he held on with all his strength. I knew that he was holding on for me, too.

"You're right," Paps said, "This could take forever. Hey, Matthew go and fetch the longer ropes and just hang 'em." Paps spoke words of pure evil. How could he live with himself?

I overheard someone say, "Why doesn't he just say he did it." Wull, for one thing he wouldn't confess to something he didn't do— I knew Jones too well. I got choked up inside, and I felt a tear roll down my cheek for the first time and I said, "Because he's a man."

The rope for the hanging was all ready. Paps put the whip down and was going to let Phillip and Matthew finish his job. As they put the rope around his neck, Jones looked at me and he looked deep into my eyes. I had dreams all my life about the way he looked at me then. He mouthed the words "until heaven." I shut my eyes tight as the rope was pulled and he was hanged. I knew by the gasps of everyone that he was dead, but I didn't want to open my eyes. I didn't want to believe it. When I did open my eyes again, he was already on the ground. They had cut the rope. All of a sudden, the sky clouded up and it began to pour. It was as if God was angry, and I knew that He was. God's child had been killed. The rain was like a huge waterfall that kept pouring. Poor God, He was crying because one of His children was brutally killed.

"Cranby, I want him buried by the time the rain stops ya here, boy," Matthew said.

"Yes sir," Cranby responded.

I ran to Jones and knelt down next to him in the pouring rain just as the tears finally started coming down. I shook him. I shook him to get up.

"Jones, Jones you can get up now... they, they all gone," I whispered to him. "Please Jones, please." I lay my head on his chest and began to bawl. I leaned my head back in the rain screaming, "Why! Oh dear God why!" I couldn't stop crying. Soon I was in Emma's arms crying. We both sat there right in the middle of the rain not moving for anything in the world. I cried and cried. I cried for all the times I pushed back my tears. I cried for my family. I cried because my soul mate was dead on the ground. I cried because it wasn't me lieing on the ground.

Before I went back inside, Emma cleaned me a up a little. She tried to get off all the dirt that was on my face. I walked in the house and into the living room with my heart torn out. It felt like someone shoved nails inside my stomach. Each step I took my legs grew heavier and heavier. The three ladies were up and having their usual chat in the living room.

"Tears over a nigger. It's hard to believe you didn't have some sort of sick relations going on." Mama said.

"No, Mama, that's not it at all. When you know someone, friend or not, and you see them beaten nearly to death and then hanged and do not shed a tear. . . well, then, may God have mercy on your soul," I said, feeling the tears roll down my cheeks. I quickly ran up to my room.

"Good, run up ro your room," She snickered.

I didn't come out of my room for the next two days. I didn't budge much for that matter. On the third day, Lily told me that I should go on outside and visit Jones's grave. I thought that it sounded like a good idea. I got up and went outside to where the slave graveyard was. I saw Jones's right away, and tears fell as I walked towards it. I sat down next to him and began to talk.

"Jones, I really miss you not being here. Just the fact that I know I will never be able to see you again is what hurts so bad. It's only been a couple of days, but I will have to deal with this my whole life." I patted the ground where he laid. I soon began to talk to him like he was still alive. I would have to catch myself from carrying on about something or another. I would start rambling. I heard someone coming up behind me. I quickly turned around and saw that is was Emma. I wiped my eyes roughly to make it look like my eyes were itching when in reality I was wiping my tears away.

"Um, uh… hey Emma," I said stumbling for words.

"Sweetheart, ya don'ts have ta hide dose tears. There is nothin' wrong with cryin' cause someone dies, especially when ya loved dem so. Infacts its quite healthy. When I's used ta tell ya not ta cry whats I meant was ya can't go cryin' every time somethang not goin' ya way. Or when someone is pickin' on ya, ya shouldn't cry; ya should be strong. I was just tryin' ta gets ya to be stronger on da inside. Whens ya lose someones ya love they ain't nothing wrong with cryin'." She grabbed and held me. Lying my head on her shoulder I let the tears come out, and they wouldn't stop. Before she left, she told me that Jones would want me to go and live a happy life. I knew that she was right. I couldn't go on mourning forever.

That night I tried it again, looking in the mirror. Except the only difference was I didn't try so hard. I didn't have any strength left. I just stared without trying. For the first time, I saw myself—what was really underneath my skin. I saw a person of hope, perseverence, and determination. I saw all that through the mirror looking deep into my eyes. I knew right then and there that everything was going to fall into place and somehow be alright. I knew I was going to make it. My heart jumped because it was such a blessing. That night I didn't sleep alone because I knew Jones was with me and would always be.

Chapter 28

Word was getting round Albany that the Wadsworth plantation had a nigger lover. When Paps and Mama found out about that, they were furious. They couldn't· hurt their reputations and let people think that there was a nigger lover in the home. Paps was looking for a place that I could go off to school and stay there and get a good education. It just so happened that the place was all the way up north in Maine, which was as far away as they could get me. My parents were giving up a child rather than to hurt their name. I was to leave Thursday morning.

Wednesday morning I thought I would get started with all my goodbyes. A goodbye is one of the hardest words to say. I find it harder than saying you're sorry. Sure, you might have to lower your pride to say sorry, but goodbyes could be forever. I walked over to Pete and told him goodbye. He reached down to my level and hugged me.

"Izzy, I just want to say that Jones, wherever he is, he's in a happier place because he cain't suffers no mo'e. Tries to think of it likes that," Pete said trying to make good of something bad.

"You're right, Pete," I said understanding what he meant.

"Let's race one last time Izzy," Pete said.

"You got it," I said taking off with him behind me. We raced to the cotton field which was about hundred and fifty yards away.

"Thanks," I said catching my breath.

"For what?" Pete said.

"For letting me win," I said.

And Pete just smiled and we hugged one last time.

I walked over to Ticey and Cranby and told them goodbye. They hugged and held me one at a time. Ticey had tears in her eyes because she already had to see Junior go and now I was leaving, too.

I, then, went to Ole Uncle, and I hugged him without saying anything at first. He picked me up of the ground, and I squeezed him even harder.

"I's gonna miss ya, Izzy," Ole Uncle said as a tear rolled down my cheek.

"I'm gonna miss you, too."

"Bye my sugar," Ole Uncle said putting me back on the ground.

"Bye Ole Uncle," I said as we departed.

I saw Joe and Sam walking by, and even though neither of them wanted anything to do with me, I told them goodbye anyway. I had no response except the slightest nod from Joe. I didn't let that bother me. I figured it was their loss. I ran to Emma where she was working in the cotton fields. She saw me coming and yelled for me.

"Come here baby!" Emma called to me. I was in those arms before you knew it. I thought that we would never part. I felt so safe, so protected in those arms. Emma would try to do anything she could form me to be safe and protected.

"Dontcha ever forget me, Izzy. Promise me ya won't ever forget me," Emma said holding onto me.

"How could I? Emma, how could you even think for a second I would ever forget you. You're my best friend. Emma how could…" I couldn't finish what I was saying. I just kept hugging her.

"Izzy, dear sweet Izzy." She looked at me like a mother looks at a child.

"Emma, oh Emma, I love you. I love you so much Emma. I wish that you could come with me."

"Izzy, I's messed ups. I's darn messed ups." She said as slow as molasses.

"What? How'd you mess up?" I asked not sure what she was talking about.

"Izzy, I gots too attached, and nows it's gonna's be mo'e dan hell, mo'e dan hell to see yous go. Emma said with gloomy eyes because she realized now she was in a way losing another child.

There were no words I could say to express how much Emma meant to me. I grabbed her shoulders and pulled her close to me and we held one another. I remember looking into her eyes, and I swore I saw a tear as she said go and tell Jones bye. And for the first time ever, Emma let a tear fall down her face. That made me realize what an important role I played in her life because she loved me as much as I loved her.

I made my way slowly to the graveyard where Jones lay. I moved towards Jones's grave and pulled a letter out that was in my pocket. I began to read it to him. It read:

Dear Jones,

It's so hard for me to see you like this. It hurts so much. I took a long walk in the cornfields, but I couldn't manage to fly or even run not without you. Jones, I miss you terribly. There is not a minute that goes by that I do not think about you. Jones, you were are my soul mate and I know we will always be together somehow. We are too strong for that. No one will be able to take you out of my memory. Now that I lost you, I have to leave Emma and everyone else cause Paps and Mama are sending me up North. They sending me as far away as they possibly could, so it seems.

Oh, Jones, I ain't ever going to find anyone quite like you. No one's ever going to be able to replace you. Jones, I will try to walk in your way. I have remembered everything you have taught me, and I will use it to teach others. I'm sad that you are gone and away from me, but Jones, no more tears in heaven. For you will not get beaten, you will see no hatred. There, in heaven, lies only love and peace. I am happy for you. I love you and will always remember you. Please, don't forget me in heaven. Until heaven

Jones, remember, until heaven.

Love,

Izzy

I dug up a little hole and put the letter there so Jones could have it forever. Tears rolled down my cheeks as I looked at the ground where his body would remain. I raised my head up at the sky and asked God why. Why to an innocent man whom you loved? I didn't understand why he would let a good and righteous man die like that in such pain. It didn't seem right; it didn't seem fair. Someone whom I needed, whom I loved was taken from me in such an awful and painful way. I later learned that God gave men their own free will and men did things that God hated, and He had to sit and watch.

That night I had everything packed into my suitcases and ready to leave the next morning. It hurt that I was being forced to leave because a "nigger lover" wasn't wanted. How disgusted I was. It was hard to think that because you treated people as equals you were to be forced out your home. I was unwanted by my family who lived inside my house, but my family who lived outside longed for me to stay. I looked out my window to the fields where I had made all my dreams, all my wishes—where I flew. I was leaving all of it. I didn't want to go; I wanted to stay at my home, at my fields. Sure, I complained about my relatives, but I didn't want to leave any of them. I knew we never got along or anything but leave, to be alone I was scared. I did not know anyone outside Macon, and I did not want to go.

Lily pulled the covers up to my neck for the last time. It was the last time I would sleep in my bed and I knew it. I knew if I ever came back it wouldn't be for good. I wasn't wanted. I was the intruder—the different one. Why, God, why do we see so differently? Do your eyes see the truth or is it the heart that knows righteousness?

Chapter 29

The next morning, Lily woke me up for the last time along with Ann.

"Izzy, wake up sweetie." Lily shook me. Although I was already awake, when she shook me I didn't open my eyes. I just lay there. I didn't want to get up, but I did anyway. I got up and got ready to leave the only place I ever lived. I told my goodbyes to Lily and Ann. Lily was crying when I hugged her, and I noticed myself start up, too. I walked down the stairs for the last time and looked at my family. The three ladies were in the living room with Joseph playing on the floor. They were just going on like a regular day. I think that Joseph was still mad at me. They didn't stand up to say goodbye. Since there was a chance that I might never see them again, I hugged them all, but there was no warmth, no meaning behind the hug. The hugs were more icy and sharp. I told them that I loved them. I knew I didn't have any connections with any of them, but I did love them for I think we tried to get along. We just couldn't connect; we didn't blend. I still don't believe I was lying when I told them I loved them; I believe, I hope I was speaking the truth.

Charles got the bags and put them in the buggy. I was surprised to see that Sam was driving instead of Pete. My Paps was going to accompany me. I walked out onto the porch, and sighed looking at the cornfield where me and Jones spent our time together. I saw that another buggy was right next to ours, and I was wondering who it was for. Then I realized that it was Mrs. Brownson. She walked over to me with a jolly smile.

"I just had to tell you goodbye before you left. Now, Isabel, you are a very special person, and I always thought this of you. And remember to be strong, be **strong**," Mrs. Brownson said emphasizing the word strong. She handed me some of her delicious cookies because she thought they would be useful on the way up.

"Thanks Mrs. Brownson, thank you very much," I said. She hugged me and off she went. When she told me to be strong, it reminded me of the time I told Junior to be strong on his journey, and now I must be strong on mine.

Paps was in the buggy waiting for me. I guess he thought the least he owed me was "a moment" because he didn't rush me. I started running closer to the fields. It felt as if a hundred pairs of eyes were watching me. I suddenly stopped and threw my arms in the air and on the top of my lungs I yelled goodbye and that I loved everyone. Emma was smiling as if she was proud, and Mama had about lost it by then. Oh shoot, that felt good just to let that out. It felt good to be the opposite of a "lady" in front of the three perfect southern ladies. If they would have ever tried the outside world, I know for a fact they would have never gone back to drinking tea at noon and eating cake on dollies. If they would have really looked at how beautiful nature was they couldn't have missed one day of God's work.

I saw Emma waving her hand to me as I left the Wadsworth plantation. I waved farewell to the plantation and to everyone at home, my home.

When we arrived into town, there was a stagecoach waiting to bring me to South Carolina. There, I would get on a locomotive headed for Maine, where I would go to school. Paps got my luggage on the stage coach, and as I was about to get off I turned to Sam and said, "I wish I would of known you better."

Sam just nodded.

I walked up to the stagecoach when I heard my name being called. I turned around and there stood my guardian angel, Miss Laura, and I ran to her and hugged her.

"You weren't gonna leave without telling me goodbye."

I shrugged and hugged her again. "I'm sorry."

"Izzy, don't let this change your heart. Don't you ever let go of that determination. Keep that heart of fire and strong will and you will make it through everything. Promise me Isabel."

"I won't let go," I said, "Oh, and Miss Laura, thank you, thank you for everything. I know I'm going to some academic school where there will these scholarly teachers, but Miss Laura I will never ever have a teacher like you. I mean that with all of my heart." She smiled, and she shut her eyes for she knew I might never return.

"Isabel you have been a blessing in my life and I think I will miss you more than I have ever missed anyone. I thank you Isabel, for you, too, taught me great lessons that I will cherish." She held on to my hands and put them on her heart. "Oh, Izzy you are truly a gift. I do not want you to leave, but I believe everything happens for a reason. And for whatever strange reason this is for, it will only make you stronger." Miss Laura smiled and pulled me close to her chest and held me.

"Isabel, you have to get on the stage coach now," Paps said. Surprisingly enough Paps let go of his pride and patted me on the shoulder.

"Bye, Miss Laura. Thank you for everything," I said walking away backwards toward the stage coach.

"Bye my love," Miss Laura responded with her hands reached out toward me.

As I was on the stagecoach I stood up and said goodbye. "Goodbye everyone! Goodbye! Goodbye Georgia! Goodbye, my sweet Georgia! Goodbye!"

Chapter 30

I was going on a journey that would change the rest of my life. As I was sitting in the stage coach, I was wondering how I was going to manage without Emma, Jones, or Miss Laura. How was I going to manage without the comfort of the fields? Who would I turn to? I grew more afraid of what awaited in Maine. I thought about running away, going off to another plantation just so I could lay in wind of the south. I, then, remembered I had to be brave and not run away from my fears. I had to be brave as Jones was.

I gazed out the window looking at the horizon as we drifted further north to a new place, a new home. I was wondering if I would fit in with the other people my age. I never had a companion that was the same age as myself. My companions were much older. Only a few hours into the journey and I already missed the smell of the house, the smell of the food, the smell of cornfield. I must be strong I told myself remembering Mrs. Brownson's words. I wanted to be strong like Jones was strong and Emma; I tried to be as strong as they had been.

We rode straight through the night and I didn't shut my eyes once. I couldn't; I was too anxious, too alone, too angry. When I started to feel bad for myself, I would think of Jones, Emma, and the rest of the slaves how everyday they lost something. I kept trying to tell myself that I might be better off in Maine. I thought I could have a better home, but I couldn't think how I could make a home complete without my three favorite companions. I had to be strong and fight my battles like Odysseus. He was a strong warrior on his journey and I had to be too.

As the sun was rising, we pulled over to rest the horses and for the driver to sleep. We stopped in a small town not too far from South Carolina. I still wouldn't sleep. At that point, I could have laid my head down and fallen asleep for days, but I wouldn't let myself. I had to many thoughts running through my head. Plus, I feared if I would sleep again, I would have nightmares of Jones's death— now that the reality of it all has hit me. I got out my journal and began to write. I wrote how I was scared that I would continue to feel the absence of love and warmth. I wrote my feelings on having to say goodbye to Georgia.

Chapter 31

The few days it took to reach Charleston, South Carolina, felt like months. When I departed from the driver, I felt bad because I was not my normal self. He seemed like a nice, decent man, but I didn't engage in any conversation. He tried to start quite a few, but with my one word responses he stopped. Any other time, I was sure we would have talked the entire time and then it wouldn't have seemed like such a long trip. For some reason, I couldn't manage to speak; I just couldn't.

Never in my life had I seen a locomotive, and when I saw the form of transportation I was going to take, I grew my first smile since my departure from Georgia. I had never seen anything like it. It was... well, I must say it was amazingly wonderful. Waiting for the locomotive to be ready to board, I sat on a bench next to a woman who appeared to be very elegant and high class. She wore a bright red dress and a matching hat which was covered with bird feathers along the edges. I laughed as I saw a man in a suit with quarter-size-gold buttons going horizontally down his navy blue suit wave his hat in the air to holler "all aboard!"

I grabbed on to the slightly chilled, shiny metal pole that led up the steps inside the locomotive. I walked slowly on to the red carpeted floor and found the seat close to the back next to a window. I giggled as I looked at what I was in, a locomotive.

We soon took off and headed toward New York. The locomotive did not run all the way to Maine so I would have to ride another stage coach to get there. I looked out my window onto the land we were speeding so swiftly away from. I longed for the land, the grass looked so gorgeous, and yet I was speeding swiftly away from it all. I was speeding further away from my home.

A young man pushing a cart walked by asking if he could give any of the passengers tea or coffee. I, of course, did not want either but asked for milk instead. I pulled out another of

Mrs. Brownson's cookies and tasted the sweetness as I bit into it. While gulping down my milk and finishing off my second cookie, I noticed all the people in their seats either reading, talking to a new acquaintance they met on the trip, or just staring off into space letting their mind play. I stared carefully at everyone, watching their moves. One man was shaking his leg constantly; a woman was twirling her hair with the tips of her fingers. They could have been anxious, angry, or alone like me, or maybe they were both just habits formed at an early age. As I stared at these strangers, I realized how they all had stories of their own. These stories, could have been happy, bliss, colorful lives, or they might have been dark, damp, and grey with only tears. These strangers might have been familiar with a loss like mine, losing your soul mate, then your home.

I finally grew the courage to sleep. Maybe it wasn't courage— just the fact that I could not keep my eyes open any longer. Thankfully, I did not have a nightmare. I didn't even dream of my leaving Georgia or Jones's death. I dreamt I was still with Jones. I dreamt of the two of us laying in the cornfields in our special spot. We just talked and talked like we used to. It was beautiful. The dream was so real to me that I could feel the corn stalks tickling my back. I felt the sun shining on my nose, and I heard Jones's voice, his powerful yet compassionate voice echoing in my ears and in my soul. I wished for the whole experience to be real, but when I awoke from an extremely long sleep I realized my perfect dream was just in fact a dream. I realized how I would never be able to see or hear Jones again except in my dreams.

Chapter 32

We soon reached New York City, and I'll tell you that place was like a different world compared to the South. I did not mind it so much because the place did have its own beauty. Sure, you wouldn't see a plantation or a beautiful cornfield, but the city had beauty. I wished Jones and Emma could have seen New York City. I wished they could have seen what my eyes showed me. I saw a man, a black man dressed in a suit walking into a tall building. He looked and walked like a business man. He was not being treated like an animal. Some men there might have thought of him to be less important but not all men. I wanted to run over to him and shake his hand and say, "Congratulations, you've crossed the impossible line." I wanted to talk with him. Instead, I smiled and said, "How do you do?"

He, this man stared into my eyes as if he were trying to read them and responded with a tip of his hat, "Fine, Miss, have a lovely day." He spoke very dignified and in a complete business manner.

As he passed, I threw my head back and laughed, thinking how Mama and Paps would have had a fit. I thought how they would have been pulling their teeth out if they saw anyone not of their own race becoming very successful. I thought how maybe one day everything will fall into place, one day.

I soon found the man who would be taking me to Portland, Maine, where I would start a new life. The trip didn't seem half as long because this time I chatted with the driver and I slept once again. I slept and had wonderful dreams.

Chapter 33

After sometime, I finally reached Maine. I felt lost as I assumed I would; I didn't know anyone. Their culture and surroundings were very different than the simple ways of the South. I was in a different world, yet like New York City, Portland, too, had its own beauty. Maine had protested against slavery. I was thrilled I would never have to witness what I did on my plantation. There was ocean surrounding the land. Ocean I had never seen before; ocean that was as blue and beautiful as you see in your dreams. Ocean that I later danced in. Ocean that became my cornfield in Maine. Although the land was much different, it was the same big blue sky that me and Jones shared, and the same sun hung above me. I soon felt like for the first time since I left Georgia I was going to be alright.

An elderly women by the name of Mrs. Wharton, who wore spectacles and smelled of cinnamon, and who was more keen to look at than to speak with took me into my new school and my new home. Mrs. Wharton was a very strict woman who taught us manners and discipline. At first, I was not fond of her at all because of her sarcastic and blunt personality, but slowly I realized how special she really was. When I thought that she was being rude or critical, she was actually being quite helpful. She, too, grew a liking to me and was pretty upset I did not pursue a career in teaching as did so many of the girls at the Portland Dormitory for Women.

The first few months I wrote many letters home, yet I would never get one in return. I felt bad when Wednesdays came and all the students dashed to the mail room to see what their parents or friends had to say or what care package they sent.

"Peterson... Smith!... package for Johnson!... Miller...another package for Brown!... " The person would yell reading out the list of mail. I never once heard my name, and for the first few months I waited, foolishly hoping maybe, just maybe, a letter bore my name. I was let down every time.

I recall one day a girl, Susan Jennings, whom I didn't like too much sarcastically asked, "Gosh, Wadsworth, your family must really like you. Have they sent you one letter? What did you do, kill them?" I didn't respond to Susan; I just looked at her and sighed.

It took me a while to make a friend. Part of me couldn't quite share a close friendship with anyone. To get too close to anyone, I figured would bring upon too much pain. I was too shy to these strange faces, these strange voices. No one sounded like they did down in Georgia. At first, my only friends were my books. My books were the only things I could count on and understand. Well, my books and my music. There was a gorgeous, antique piano which I tried to play every second I could. The music teacher, Mrs. Carmichael, was an extremely energized woman who believed it was music that will change the lives of her young students. I believed her, too. Her only love in the world was the melody of the instruments.

Chapter 34

As spring turned in to fall and fall to winter, I was growing more and more fond of Maine. I was growing to be a stronger individual as Miss Laura said I would. Winters in Maine were terribly freezing, yet I found the beauty in the cold, and I twirled in the snow. I began to find beauty in most things since my arrival in Maine, for beauty was surrounding my very essence, my soul. When I grew lonely in the cold nights, I found comfort in the moon. This may sound foolish, but I talked to the moon. I talked to the moon as if it were Jones. Jones was my man in the moon. For the moon was so bright, making sure there was never complete darkness, and I felt that it was Jones making sure I had enough light in my lonely nights.

I was not always alone, for I made friends–people I could laugh with and talk too. I guess I didn't want to get too close to anyone; I suppose one could say I was scared, scared to have a close friends again. Losing my companions in Georgia was the hardest event I had been through, and although I was growing stronger, I was not yet strong enough.

I soon stopped writing so many letters back home. I didn't find the meaning in doing it any longer. I wrote over ten letters asking them to send me Miss Laura's address, but I never received a response.

Before I knew it, I had been in Maine for six years. Six years of my life drifted away from me, and I finished with my schooling at the age of twenty two. Many of my friends became teachers because a teacher along the road inspired them somehow, and now they wished to share their creativity, their skills with others, to inspire. They wanted to express their love of knowledge with students of their own. I, then, thought of Miss Laura, one of the best teachers I ever had. If I was going to become a teacher, I wanted to be like her. I considered becoming a teacher for a while because I wanted to inspire others to love to learn. Only I did not become one because I fell in love. I wanted a family, and I chose the love of this man over the love of teaching.

Chapter 35

I was sitting alone, treating myself to a refreshing glass of lemonade at Shiny Bob's Diner, a place I would often go to. As I was sipping my drink and flipping through a book, I saw the man I would later fall in love with through the corner of my eye. The man had dusty brown hair that fell of to one side of his face, eyes as green as the grass in Georgia, and a smile that made your knees weak. He had a thousand different smiles, and I memorized every single one of them.

When I saw him drawing closer to me, I grew nervous for I feared a loss of words. I thought I would have nothing to say to him.

"May I join you?" The man asked casually.

"Yes, of course," I said shutting my book.

"I hope I'm not interrupting anything?" He asked pointing to my book.

"Oh gosh no." I laughed thinking that I had already read the book twice before. I was reading it again because I wanted to find more meaning to the words. I always seemed to hear more beauty in the words the second or third time of reading a book.

"If you don't mind me asking Miss, what is a beautiful lady like yourself sitting here all alone?" He asked with one of his thousands of smiles.

How was I supposed to respond to that? I blushed because I rarely received complements on my beauty. My head was down facing the table and as I lifted it I said, "My name is Isabel, Isabel Wadsworth.

He smiled even bigger and responded, "William, William Climmings."

Well, five minutes turned to an hour, and an hour into three. He was very easy to talk with. I felt myself opening up to him more than I did with anyone in six years. We spent three hours flirting, complementing one another, and discussing dreams and aspirations. I didn't mention too much about Georgia just the fact that I had once lived there. I think he knew Georgia was a tender subject for me to speak of.

That night, I remember I could hardly sleep. I kept thinking of this man, this man who seemed flawless. I was so thankful I went to Shiny Bob's Diner that day for I almost passed it up to go with Mrs. Wharton to the library, but for some reason I didn't go that day. I always wonder if it was fate telling me not to go.

William and I spent lots of time with each other. We could barely stand to be apart. We would take long walks on the beach letting the waves splash upon our feet and watch the sunset. We would go to the top of the lighthouse and look up at all the stars and whisper our love for one another. We would memorize one another's faces with the touch of our hands. We would always dance to the songs of the birds and lie in the wild flowers and allow the petals and pollen to cover us. The more we were falling for each other the more afraid I became.

William and I had a lot in common. We felt the same way about slavery, about how the color of someone's skin does not determine their power, their worth. We both loved the beauty of nature and meaning of words in books. We had vivid imaginations and strong wills. We liked the joy and sorrow of music and the comfort of the ocean. More importantly we had fallen completely in love with one another. We treated each other as royalty. I never thought I would find a man that felt the same way about life as I did, but I was lucky, but I don't think luck is the right word to use. Each day I spent with William, we grew closer together.

I didn't admit it to him at the time, but I was scared of getting to close. I soon grew over it when I realized how much I loved him. We were sitting on the itchy white sand looking out to the sun as it was setting. The sun looked like it was going into the water as it lowered for the evening. Our hands were tightly rapped in between our arms as we admired our scenery.

"Isabel, you know what I love about you?" William asked as he gently put back some of my hair that had flown to the front of my face.

"What?" I wasn't in the mood to guess.

"I love the fact that your not like most girls. You don't hide your feelings, your not confusing nor predictable, your aggressive, and you've stolen my heart. No girl has ever done that before. Your special." He looked at me with a tilt of his head and kissed my cheek.

I quickly looked at him and faked a smile; I was nervous. I was scared I was beginning to actually love William too. I knew I loved him, but I was scared that I was getting too attached. If I were to lose him or if he were to lose me–one of us would be left in a great deal of pain. I didn't want that for either of us.

"Isabel, you know this could be forever."

"What?" I knew what he was talking about I just didn't want to believe it.

"Us, we could last forever, our relationship." He looked at me with a smile of pure happiness.

I shook my head, stood up, and began running. I didn't know where I was running to, but I was running. I was running away from my fears like I was always told not to do.

William started following me shouting my name out for me to come back. I didn't turn around I was to scared.

William soon caught up with me and grabbed my shoulders. "Gosh, your fast," He said catching his breath. "William, please let me go. I have to go and think." I was desperate.

"Wait, please Isabel just for a minute." William sounded more desperate. "Look, we both love each other. I know that for a fact, and I also know that you are scared to love me. I know someone or something has hurt you in the past, and I'm guessing your pain is from Georgia since you rarely speak of it. I'm not asking you to talk about it and I understand that is very hard. Isabel, I promise I won't hurt you, but please just don't push me away," William said as he looked deep into my eyes and then held in my arms as I wept.

"I'm sorry. Oh, William I'm sorry. I have been hurt in the past, and I haven't gotten close to anyone since. I fear if I get too close, then…"

William wouldn't let me finish. "You won't get hurt. I won't let you." We embraced again, and then William kissed me like he never did before.

Chapter 36

One evening William asked me to meet him at the top of the lighthouse. I figured we would just admire the stars and one another, but the particular evening was much more special. As I walked up to the top of the lighthouse, William was there waiting for me with a white and red rose, and he wore a smile that was filled with excitement.

"Isabel, these are for you," he paused for a second and then went on, "the white rose symbolizes your pure heart and soul, and the red rose symbolizes your warmth, compassion, and my love for you. Isabel, I find myself growing more in love with you as the days go by." He placed his hands in mine and said, "Isabel, will you make me the happiest man in the world by being my wife." Our eyes locked, and I leaned towards his lips and kissed them for he had made me completely happy.

He looked at me as if he was waiting for an answer, and I laughed and told him, "Well, that was a yes, William. I cannot think of anything better than for you to be my husband."

July 28, 1842 the most wonderful and beautiful day of that year. I was dressed in a white gown walking towards my groom. My groom who seemed to be the happiest man in all of Maine. We held each others hands the entire ceremony. It was a small ceremony and very untraditional, in fact some people in Portland didn't approve. William and I really weren't concerned with the opinions of others on our very special day. We had our wedding outside near the beach and the lighthouse where we fell in love; we thought our wedding spot was very appropriate. Many people felt that it was wrong to get married outside of the church, but William and I actually felt God's presence more among nature, His own work.

We prepared vows in order to voice our love for each other. I was first to say my vows which I had rewrote and practiced over hundred times.

"William, I never thought I would find love as precious and as true as Juliet's, but I have. I have found the man whom I will love and cherish for the rest of my life. You have touched my life in many ways. You have made my journey in life have meaning once again. From the first time I met you, you have touched my heart, and I am more than happy to know you will continue to move me with the beauty of your words and the beauty of your soul. I never really understood what it meant, to fall in love, until I met you, William." William never cried the entire time we were married except when I said that, but I didn't find my vows as moving as his.

"I never knew love until I saw you for I knew somehow you'd change my life for the better. Isabel, there are no words that can express how wonderful you are, and there are no words to express how deeply in love I am with you. I would rather spend one day with you than do anything else in the world, for one touch of your lips is worth all the money in the world. You are the treasure I have been searching for, and you are worth more to me than my own soul. I would be lost without you in my life. I dedicate my life to you, and I will be your husband until the end of time. Isabel, I am completely and forever yours, my darling, my beloved.

His words moved me to tears because I never knew he loved me that much. When we both said "I do" our hearts became united. I thought how proud and happy Jones, Emma, and Miss Laura would be that I found a man like William to share my life with.

I knew Jones was watching from heaven my joyous day; I just wished Emma and Miss Laura could have seen me. I felt I had been suspended in time during the years before I met William, weaving and unweaving my tapestry–waiting for my true love. At the end of the long road of despair, such love swallowed me whole.

Chapter 37

Our house was in an extremely close vicinity to the lighthouse and the ocean. The house was perfect, centered in the middle of the most extraordinary wild flowers, black-eyed Susans, buttercups, and golden-rods. They smelled as wonderful as they looked. I would sometimes lay alone in the flowers and fall asleep among their delicate petals until William would awake me with a kiss upon my lips.

William was a fisherman because he loved the ocean and being on the water made him content. When he was away, I would visit Georgia in my mind. I ran to the beach and would jump into the chilly water and visit Georgia. As I was swimming, I thought about the conversation Jones and I had once about how the first one of us who learned how to swim was suppose to teach the other. Where was Jones so I could teach him how to swim? Where was my soul mate? Seven years ago Jones passed away and not a single day went by where I didn't think of him. Georgia and the friendships I made their were always on my mind.

When William was fishing and I was lonely, I found comfort and protection from the salty water ocean. Her waves eased my mind as I floated passed the shore. It was a time for me to enjoy the solitude because even though I had a life-long companion I still thought it necessary to have privacy. Solitude allows one to have inner thoughts not to be shared with others.

Soon, three glorious years of marriage passed, and William and I were still infatuated with each other. Our third year of marriage was our best because we received the most precious gift possible, a child. We had a baby whom we named Jones. William never asked me why I wanted so badly to name our son Jones, and I never told. I still kept Georgia in my heart. I knew if I started speaking of my past I would cry and begin to feel empty again. I still kept the journal from Georgia, and I read it often remembering my friends, the joys and sorrows of Macon.

It was all so clear to me; when I closed my eyes, I would remember back and see the plantation. The memories were like a painting.

I treasured my baby. He was the sunshine in my life. You see my baby was born blind and it killed me. I thought my baby will never get to see all the wonderful things God made. The perfect blue sky, the colorful birds, the clear blue ocean, everything William and I took for granted. Then again, it was sort of a blessing in disguise that he was born this way because my baby would never see hatred. He could never judge someone by the color of their skin; he would have to get to know the person, just the way we taught him. The years went by and little Jones was growing up to be quite a man. I always made sure that he had enough love and affection. I always made sure that he behaved himself; we made him realize how much his parents cared for him and cherished him. I taught him all the things that Jones, Emma, and Miss Laura had taught me.

You hear people say that having a child is a miracle, and you nod your head for you imagine it is. People are wrong; having a child is much, much more than a miracle. With God's help, you, yourself, in someway had a part in creating a beautiful life. When I first held my baby Jones in my arms, I was hooked. I was already in love with this perfect creature.

When your baby, no matter what age is hurt by someone's words or someone's hands your heart aches worse than your own child's. I would rather take all his pain in order to spare him any suffering. It was too painful and troublesome for me and William to see him hurt. I began to think how cruel people were to one another. It's amazing how people make fun of what is different either for a few laughs or because they are afraid of anything beyond ordinary. The truth of it all is, ordinary could possible be the worst thing to be.

Little Jones grew up too fast. One minute we were teaching how to walk and before you know it we were celebrating his eleventh birthday. Along with the year of Jones's eleventh birthday came my thirty-sixth birthday. I had lived twenty years of my life in Maine, and I spent fourteen of those years married to William. Although I lived in Maine longer than Georgia, I still missed Georgia and felt more comfortable calling that place home. Don't ask why? I had a great life in Maine, and I was extremely content. I guess, I just felt something missing. When I looked out the window, I would see Georgia. I saw Jones and Emma working in the fields. I would smell Lily and Ann cooking up a storm. I closed my eyes and pictured myself flying through the fields with Jones. I would remember Miss Laura, my teacher and my friend, picking up a new book, an adventure for me to read or another paper for me to write. Every time I picked up a book I would remember the words Miss Laura spoke to me about a book–the words within them, what they meant, what they were, and how you must read between the lines.

Soon I just couldn't place myself; I couldn't think. I was very confused, but I knew what I needed to do. I was going on an adventure. It was twenty years since I last stood on Georgia soil, and it was time I went back to visit. I felt that it would be best if I traveled alone when I went back so I could really think and clear my mind. I think that I needed to be alone. It reminded me of Odysseus's arrival back home twenty years later. Odysseus went back home and people didn't believe that it was him they thought he was dead. I knew my family did not think I was dead, but in a way I was already dead to them. When I said goodbye to Georgia, it was as if I had died to them that moment. Odysseus's wife soon realized that the man who stood before her was her husband she had been longing for. I feared that I might not have anyone who cares that I am back.

Chapter 38

When I arrived in Georgia, I asked a man if he would take me to the Wadsworth plantation. The whole experience was terribly awkward going back to my childhood and adolescent years. Even though everything was the same my home seemed much grayer then I remembered it. I first walked to the graveyard to see Jones's grave. Scanning the yard, I noticed quite a few plots had been added. I saw Ole Uncles's, Joe's, sweet Lily's, Ann's and Cranby's. The people who had a major part in forming my characteristics, my personality, my strength– these people held a part in molding me, and I never got to thank them. I never even got to tell them goodbye. Tears rolled down my cheeks as memories of these friends went through my head.

I walked toward the cornfield. I noticed people starring at me because they had no idea who I was. They just thought I was a stranger walking in their fields, but they were walking in mine. Who were these people I thought; where were Emma, Jones, Lily, Cranby, and Ticey. Where were my friends. I can't tell you how I felt going back to this place. When I made it to me and Jones's special spot, it lifted my heart. I knew that I had to fly with my own wings. I started running as fast as I could through the corn field. Despite the fact that I was much slower than I was twenty years ago, I spread my wings, and I flew. The other slaves were staring at me because they had no idea what I was doing, but I didn't care. I felt like I did twenty years ago. I shut my eyes, and I was a young girl again. I felt refreshed, reborn as I was flying, spreading my own wings. After I felt my wings were reattached, I stopped abruptly because I heard my name being called.

"Izzy, Izzy, is that you?" No one had called me that since I left Georgia. Slowly, I turned around.

"Ticey?" I said questioning myself.

She ran up to me, "I can't believe it's you Izzy. My how you's grown ups." When I I looked at her, I saw the twenty year old I remembered, but she was in her forties now. We talked for a while, and I told her about Jones and William. She told me how Lily, Ann, Ole Uncle, and Cranby died. She also told me about my Grandma—how she died ten years ago. She told me that Pete had gotten sold for a younger fellow just last year. I soon held my breath and asked her about Emma. Sadly, she told me that Emma was sold about four years ago. I knew that Emma was still alive, and I knew she would live another hundred years. Emma was a rock; she was spreading the good news and her memories with others. I asked if Miss Laura still came to teach, and she told me she did. Miss Laura had finished teaching Joseph and Claire, Sarah's oldest, who was now twenty. She was now teaching Benjamin, Sarah's second child. He was around the age of sixteen. Oh, and she also told me that Mrs. Brownson and her husband had passed away too. We chatted and caught up on good times for about two hours. Surprisingly enough no one stopped us. It was as if we were in a blocked off area and no one could see us. I couldn't talk to Ticey forever I had to leave her and go inside to face my family.

I grabbed all the courage I had and walked up the porch and knocked on the door. A young striking slave that I never had seen before answered the door.

"Cane I's help ya Miss?" The lady asked.

"May I come in?" I said.

"Yes'm," The lady said.

"Thank you," I responded walking in and closing my eyes remembering the old house smell. I was walking toward the living room.

"Cane I's help ya?" The lady asked me again.

"Oh, I'm sorry. Where are my manners? Wull, you see, I used to live here. I used to call this place home," I said touching my chest where my heart was for it felt whole again.

"Isabel? Is that who you are? Ann always used to talks 'bout ร feel like I's know ya. Go rights ahead," The lady said as you do to an old friend.

118

"Thanks," I said walking into the living room. My Mama, Sarah, and a young lady who must of been Claire were sitting and drinking tea. Nothing has changed I thought to myself.

"Who are you? What do you want?" Mama asked me. I suppose she didn't recognize me.

"Hi, Mama. It's me, Isabel," I said feeling kinda funny having to tell my own Mother who I was.

"Oh, well I can tell you still have that hopeful smile. It's nice to see you again." Mama said sipping her tea. Not getting up to hug or even shake hands with her daughter she hasn't seen in TWENTY DAMN YEARS!

"It's really nice to see you again too, all of you. Golly, I feel terribly awkward. Did you ever receive any of my letters? I wrote over ten dozen. How is it that you never wrote back?" I asked a little disturbed, a little confused, a little heart-broken.

"We can hardly find the time these days to do anything at all." Mama said lying through her teeth.

I put my hand out to shake Claire's. "How are you? I'm your aunt Isabel. I'm sure you've heard some great things about me." I said sarcastically.

"Ha, I'm fine thank you, and I'm Claire." She said with a smile. She looked exactly like Sarah when Sarah was twenty.

"You know you look identical to Sarah; it's uncanny." I said taking a seat since no one offered.

"That's what I keep hearing," Claire said sipping her tea.

"Maine is beautiful, although it's not Georgia." I said to start a conversation.

Sarah nodded, "You know Isabel, your vocabulary has increased tremendously. Why, I had to get a dictionary right by me when I read your letters."

"Yes, in Maine I went to an academic school for six years. Sadly, I wasn't able to do anything with my knowledge if I wanted a family."

Changing the subject, Mama asked, "Where do you plan on staying?"

"I don't. I have a ticket for this evening." I was a little offended by that question.

"Good," Mama said, "We have a houseful as it is."

"Well, I wouldn't want to cause any trouble; I'm only family." Quickly changing the subject I asked, "How's Paps and Charles?"

"They're just fine. Papa doesn't run the plantation anymore—Joseph and Charles do," Sarah answered.

I sat and tried to think of conversations. I would ask the questions and they would answer, or I would tell them something about my life, and they would comment. It was dreadful. You think after twenty years it would take hours and hours to discuss things. When I was soon shut out of the conversation, I stood up and walked toward the library. The library door opened and out walked an elderly woman around the age of fifty. She was tall and slender, and I knew it was Miss Laura.

"Izzy, is that you?" Miss Laura was shocked. "I was beginning to think I would never see you again."

"Miss Laura," I whispered. We embraced. Tears were rolling down both of our cheeks. A couple minutes later a boy a few years older than my Jones walked out the library.

"Benjamin," Miss Laura began, "this is your aunt Isabel. She's your Mama's younger sister. Benjamin was a big eyed sixteen year old boy. His eyes were filled with curiosity.

"Nice to meet ya," He said in a polite way.

"Nice to meet you too, Benjamin," I said as he ran along.

Miss Laura and I talked for hours. She told me everything that had happened while I was away, and I told her about Maine. We laughed and cried until I had to go. I got her address so we could keep in touch. She also gave me the copy of the Odyssey which I gladly accepted. I didn't tell her, but I already had two other copies at home. I still wanted this one because it was the copy from my childhood.

he way back to Maine, I thought about my day. I did a ngs that I needed to do. My family all seemed distant from me. Joseph seemed to be a very shrewd individual. Paps was sick in bed, and I knew when I saw him he didn't have much longer although it wasn't mentioned. I thought about how sick he looked. I was for some reason the most nervous to see him. When I crawled up the stairs, my heart was beating unusually fast. As I reached his door, I held on to the tarnished gold door knob for it took quite a while to gather my thoughts on what I would say. The door slowly creaked open as I pushed it forward. Paps was awake laying down in his bed. He looked ten or fifteen years older than he was supposed to. He looked over to me as I shut the door behind me. His eyes were weak, and his face was long and had aged.

I spoke extremely slow as I said, "Paps, it's. . ."

He motioned me to the chair by the bed. My Paps, my father, who I shared nothing with was lying in a bed dying. He was feeble and beyond weak. His eyes held much pain within them; his eyes showed no strength. I could not help but feel pity for this man, I once thought of as my father. He was literally my father; I had his blood running through my veins, yet he was no figure for me to follow, to admire. Now, that he was dying my heart reached out to him.

"Paps," my voice was shaky and my heart raced even faster.

"Isabel," he said in a scratchy whisper. He looked pitiful; he looked sad. I never once saw my Paps look sad, never.

"Paps, I know it has been a long time, but I…I…" I did not know what to say to a man I hardly knew who was dying. His fingers were shriveled up altogether, and his left hand which was extremely pale reached out to mine. I placed both of my hands around his, and I allowed him to speak.

"Isabel…" he began coughing excessively, and I just patted his hand which was cupped into mine. He began again, "Isabel, I'm…I feel…I'm sor…Everything that has happened…I'm just…" He started coughing again, and I slightly squeezed his hand.

"Paps…I think I understand. I think I know what you are trying to say." My voice was cracking because I thought my

Paps was going to reconcile our differences. I was exhilarated with joy.

His eyes turned to stone, his lips quivered, and his face scrunched up together; he pulled his hand away from mine. "No...no Isabel. I can't. It's too hard..." He began coughing once again, and he let out a groan because of the pain from his body and the pain of my return. "It's been too long. It's just...It's just too late. I...I...I just can't..."

I took deep breathes and I said, "I know we never had any relationship, but Paps it is never too late. That is one thing I've learned it can never be too late."

"It's been too late!" He raised his voice and then groaned because it hurt him to yell. He grabbed his stomach and groaned.

"Please, Paps."

"It's been too long." He whispered and motioned for me to leave.

I could not plead for a reconciliation. It was not going to take place. I got up from the chair and walked to the door. Before I walked out I turned around to see the eyes of my Paps and they were filled with agony, confusion, frustration. It was an awful way to die, I thought. The man who brought a brutal death to my soul mate was now going to die more brutally. He had no love in his life. I don't know if I can call the relationship my Paps and Mama had love. For now, Paps was not going to die a man. I felt pity for him.

Although some of the confrontations I had in Georgia did not go as well as I hoped, the day did have reason. The day did have happiness. I met up with my friend, my teacher, and I grew a pair of my own wings. You see, I had to go back to Georgia because I left a piece of my heart there, and I had to go back to collect it.

Chapter 39

When I returned to Maine, I was more thankful to have William and Jones than ever before. I loved them dearly, and I was happy they were a part of me and my life. William asked why I had to go back home, to Georgia. I just told him I had to go back to see my past. I told him to read The Odyssey because it was similar to my life. He smiled on of his thousands of smiles that could light up the rainiest day.

Miss Laura and I wrote to one another until her death. She kept me up to date on just about everyone. Miss Laura was definitely a blessing in my life. She was angelic inside and out. She told me how Paps died three weeks after my visit. I then, sent a letter home saying I was going to come back down, but Mama wrote her first letter back to me telling me not to come because it would be too much trouble on my part. I thought how would it be too much trouble to go to your own father's funeral? Was I that unwanted by my own blood? I would write Ticey letters, and Miss Laura would read them to her. She would get Miss Laura to dictate letters back to me. It was nice to be able to have a form of communication from people in my past, Ticey would remind me of things I had forgotten about—things me and Jones would do. She would tell me of the songs Emma used to sing. She would remind me of the memories that were stored deep within my heart. The memories I would cry from when reminded because I missed those great days in my life. Maybe I did cry too often since I left Georgia, but I liked to think of it was if I was blessed with the gift of tears.

Soon, Miss Laura stopped writing for she grew dreadfully ill. I kept writing to her hoping someone would read her the letters to make her feel better. After a while, her niece wrote to me saying that she had passed on. What was happening I thought? Everyone I loved was dying.

After I heard of Miss Laura's death, I had reality check of life of what a miracle life really and truly is. I have been blessed to know so many wonderful people who changed my life. I would get visions of my past more often than I probably should have. I would receive hot flashes at least three or four times a day. William put me to bed early one night when I could almost smell my childhood. I feel asleep with Georgia on my mind, and I thought of Jones, my soul mate. The dream I dreamt that night was completely real I'm not sure if you are even suppose to call it a dream. I dreamt I was an old woman, older than I wished to live. I can not describe enough in detail of how real my dream was. I was telling the story of my life to a man who was fierce yet gentle. After I finished telling him my story, he had a tear rolling down his cheek. My heart jumped for it was whole once again.

"I know that tear," I whispered, "I know that tear."

The man came to me and placed me in his arms, and he whispered in my ear, "Until heaven, Izzy, until heaven."

"Jones, oh Jones!" I cried out for I missed my soul mate, the man whom I knew best. I cried out in pain for all the years he was out of my life, and I cried out in joy for he was back in my life for all eternity.

"Izzy, let's fly through the fields like old times," Jones said very calmly. I closed my eyes remembering the sound of his voice for it didn't change a bit. The man who stood before me was the man who made my life somewhat complete.

"I haven't even run in years, Jones. Look at me, I'm so old." I looked down at my hands which were covered with wrinkles and age spots. They were hands of an old woman.

"Since when have you let anything stop you," Jones said grabbing my hand which somehow turned into the hand of a child, the hand he used to hold. We walked through heaven's gates and flew through the fields together once again.

My dream was perfect; it was a perfect dream. I never wanted to wake up from it because it was all to wonderful. My dream was so real that, I don't recall if I ever woke up.

About the Author

I was fifteen years old when I finished *Goodbye Georgia*.

Born and raised in Lafayette, Louisiana. I lived in the same city and the same house until college. I met most of my friends at a relatively young age, and we have all grown up together. It's pretty special. The memories of my childhood will never leave my heart. I have left my past and my friends behind to attend a small liberal arts school in New York City. New York is becoming another home for me, although I will never forget where I come from because Louisiana is a very special place. I do not know exactly what I would like to do for the future. All I know is that I have so many different goals and dreams, I seriously hope time permits me to do them. Right now, I am in the midst of completing another novel. I think I will always continue to write because I have so many different stories and so many different characters that speak to me through my thoughts. I wish they existed so I could be with them because they are far too interesting to just be fiction.

Printed in the United States
733200002B